GATEKEEPER

CHARITY PARKERSON

--Warning: This book is intended for readers over the age of 18.

Copyright © 2017 Charity Parkerson
Editor: Hercules Editing and Consultants
Photographer: Taria Reed | The Reed Files
All rights reserved.

INTRODUCTION

HE'S A PLAYER. EVERYONE KNOWS IT. EXCEPT SEAN ISN'T A GAME TO HIM.

Mateo has been the biggest contender for the Super Lightweight title for over two years. No matter how hard he works, he can't seem to beat the current champ. Since boxing is all he has in the world, it's an issue. His confidence is in the can, and his social life is non-existent. Mateo has had no real friends or relationships that have lasted longer than one night in years. That is, until he meets a man whose beautiful heart leaves him mystified.

Rescuing a drunk from the parking lot of his workplace, Slip, isn't a new thing for Sean. People leave the bar and grill plastered and intent on driving all the time. Usually, Sean calls them a cab and sends them on their way. Mateo is the first one he's ever taken home. There's something sad about Mateo. Sean lost all his friends years ago, and he sees a kindred spirit in the sexy boxer. It's easier than he ever dreams to consider the man his best friend in no time at all. Except he's not. Mateo is so much more.

It'll take the purest heart to save a broken man from a hellish life. Unfortunately, when it comes to Mateo and Sean, it's hard to know who needs rescuing the most.

*G*atekeeper: *A fighter who other fighters challenge to establish themselves as contenders for the title.*

SLIP WAS PACKED. That wasn't unusual for a Friday night, but after the wretched day Sean had, he was over it. Nothing life altering had happened. It was more a culmination of bullshit. He'd woken up to a flat tire, making him late for class. That girl who sat two rows in front of him, the one who never shut up, had asked so many questions that his last class had spilled over. He'd been fifteen minutes late to work. Since he hadn't had time to run home and grab his "Slip" T-shirt, the manager had yelled at him, given him a new shirt, and promised it would come out of Sean's check. More money he couldn't afford to lose.

Thankfully, his section was overflowing with customers. Since he'd been informed that table seven, the one with a group of four men, had been waiting the longest, Sean tied his apron around his waist and headed their way. Despite his shit day and the even shittier manager, Sean loved working for Slip. The owners, Boston and Kaz, were amazing. Without them, he wouldn't see a single hint of light at the end of the tunnel of his dark life. They paid his high-dollar tuition at a culinary school people fought to attend. He'd only been forced to sign over his life to Slip for the next few years. Sean didn't mind. He'd given more for less before.

At the edge of table seven, Sean automatically chose the most open spot to lean across and set cocktail napkins in front of each man. "What can I get you?"

The man to his left turned in his seat. His dark eyes were sweet. They captured Sean, holding him hostage. "If I could get your phone number, I won't ask for more, and I promise to leave a huge tip."

Sean's smile was out of his control. Maybe the night wasn't a complete loss? Even better, maybe he didn't look as horrible as he felt.

The guy to his right spoke up, killing Sean's hope.

"Don't mind him. He'll fuck anything that moves. It's not personal."

The sweet dark eyes shifted, hardening. Something dark and sharp stabbed Sean in the chest. No one wanted him unless they were a piece of shit. Why couldn't he remember that? Fuck it. He'd already lost money on a T-shirt he didn't need. Sean didn't need this table. He walked away, moving to the next table without a backward glance.

Two women who looked as if they'd been drinking for hours watched his approach. Sean didn't doubt for a second his smile looked every bit as forced as it felt. "What can I get you ladies?" he asked, setting cocktail napkins in front of them.

They were both blonde—one platinum and one dark. The platinum smiled. "Another White Russian, please?"

He nodded and turned to her friend. "And you?"

"The same."

With his blatantly false smile still in place, Sean turned and ran into the hard chest of the caramel-skinned male who'd flirted with him only moments earlier. Sean's tongue froze to the roof of his mouth. Damn. The dude was even better while standing and up close. He had a good six inches on Sean and his body was hard—like a pro football star. The guy also had dimples. Sean loved dimples.

"I'm sorry about my friend," he said, and Sean's hurt slipped away. He felt it slide off like a mink coat. It was in the guy's eyes. He meant it.

Sean managed a genuine smile. "It's okay. I shouldn't have walked away. I'm just—"

"Yes, you should have," Sweet Eyes said, cutting Sean off. "Just because you're working doesn't mean you should put up with anyone's shit. I know you don't know me and have no reason to believe me, but I wasn't trying to play you."

Sean wasn't so sure that was true, but he let it slide. "I'm Sean," he said, holding out his hand.

"Mateo," his sexy new friend said, his accent thickening.

Sean had to know. "Where are you from?"

"Brazil originally, but I was raised mostly in Miami. Where are you from?" Mateo's smile said he knew his question was a ridiculous one. Sean couldn't be more obviously hometown.

"Here. My whole life," he added, in case there was any doubt. A lock of Sean's hair fell across his eyes.

Mateo pushed it behind Sean's ear. Sean's stomach quivered. It never occurred to Sean to move away, even as Mateo's gaze slid down his body. It wasn't a blatant inspection. It was better, as if Mateo couldn't resist checking Sean out. Sean hadn't felt desired in a damn long time. "If I go sit down, will you visit me again tonight?" Mateo pulled a hopeful face. "I'll let you pour a drink in my lap to make up for my friend's douchery."

A roar of laughter escaped Sean. Mateo was damn earnest—like he'd really let Sean pour a drink on him as long as he came back. Sean swiped at his eyes. "How can I resist that offer?"

Mateo's smile grew. His dimples deepened. "I'm hoping you can't."

"I have to put this drink order in before I get in trouble... again. Can I get you anything while I'm at it?"

"I'm still holding out for your number," Mateo said with a wink before walking away. Sean watched it happen with a happy inner sigh. The man did have an amazing ass and a confident walk. Sheesh. He headed for the bar before he wasted any more time. On impulse, he put in an order for a beer along with the two White Russians. He dropped the liquor off with the women and checked on his other tables before heading back to Mateo. The sexy man was sitting all alone. Sean couldn't have that. He set the beer at Mateo's elbow and claimed the empty seat next to him.

"The beer is on me. Where did your friends go?"

Mateo's gaze locked on Sean. Butterflies stirred in Sean's gut. "I have no idea. They were gone when I came back. I didn't want to risk missing you by going to look for them."

He knew he shouldn't be moved. The Mateos of the world were only out for one night of fun, but maybe that was what Sean needed. He hadn't been himself since... Well, he didn't know who he was anymore or who he'd ever been. All Sean knew was, he'd been unhappy for as far back as he could remember. He wasn't right now. Mateo made him smile.

IF MATEO WAS BEING honest with himself, he hadn't even looked at Sean before deciding to ask for his number. He'd smelled him. The man had leaned past him, setting a napkin on the table, and the slightest hint of cologne wafted over Mateo. He'd taken a shot. He could've ended up knocked out. Instead, sexy green eyes and a sweet smile had turned his way. For Mateo, it wasn't about looks. He tended to seek a personality type rather than candy. Sean wasn't that type. He would've thrown his flirt to the wind and left matters there if not for Carter's fucking mouth. Mateo didn't doubt that dude would get his teeth knocked out one day for always saying whatever he thought without a care for anyone else. Carter wasn't even his friend. Actually, Mateo didn't have friends. He had fight buddies and acquaintances. But Carter had opened his mouth, and Mateo had turned his head at just the right moment. He'd seen Sean's face before the man walked away. Mateo couldn't let him get away now.

"You bought me a drink?" Mateo wasn't sure why he was so touched by the gesture. Maybe because he wasn't nice, and people didn't do nice things for him.

Sean shrugged. "You don't want to look like a psycho, sitting here by yourself without even as much as a drink to keep you company."

Mateo couldn't stop smiling. "I think it's a toss-up. No drink and alone—psycho. Drink and alone —pathetic."

"For the moment, you're not alone. So you're neither."

But he would be in a minute when Sean went back to work. "Still, I think I'll sit at the bar."

A hint of disappointment flashed in Sean's eyes before clearing away. "Okay. I don't blame you." He stood. "Enjoy the beer."

Before he had time to think things through, Mateo grabbed Sean's arm, stopping him. "Wait. I haven't given you that huge tip I promised."

Sean winked. "Don't worry over it. I never gave you my number." Sean slipped away in the crowd before Mateo could argue.

Mateo made his way to the bar. He needed something stronger to drink.

WARM NIGHT AIR washed over Sean the second he stepped outside after his shift. He wished it would take away the scent of food and liquor. Sean closed his eyes and inhaled. His body was exhausted. Sean's mind was alive and restless, leaving him slightly dissatisfied.

"Mhmm, damn. Every time I see you, you get hotter."

Sean's eyes flew open. His heart jumped into his throat. Mateo stood nearby, looking sexy as sin and drunk as hell. He even had the drunk lean going on. "What are you doing out here?"

Mateo smiled. It was slightly goofy and endearing. "I can't find my car."

"That's probably a good thing. Did you drive here?"

Mateo cast another glance around the parking lot, seeming to think it over. He nodded, as if coming to a decision. "Yes. I drove. I remember."

Sean blew out a sigh and shook his head. In spite of himself, Sean was smiling. Even drunk, Mateo drew Sean in. "Okay. Let's go."

"Where?"

"I'll take you home."

Mateo blinked several times. Sean couldn't decide if Mateo was confused or trying to make the world stop spinning. "No. I'll wait until I remember."

"Um, no," Sean said, snagging his arm and hauling him along. "I cannot, in good conscience, let you get behind the wheel."

Mateo didn't make things easy. He dragged his feet. "I could be a serial killer or a rapist. A serial rapist," Mateo said at the top of his lungs, making Sean laugh.

Sean didn't slow. "I doubt you could get it up right now, so I'm not worried."

"You're too nice to say things like that. Plus, I could be a serial killer."

"So you've said," Sean said, unlocking his twenty-year-old car.

"I could be a rapist," Mateo said as Sean pushed him down into the passenger side seat.

"Jesus," Sean muttered as he circled the car. He probably was being stupid, but if Mateo found his car and then killed someone, Sean would have to live with it. He already had more things to live with than he could handle. Sean slid behind the wheel. Mateo had leaned the seat back. "Where do you live?"

No response came.

"Hello?" Sean called as he poked Mateo's side. "I need your address."

Nothing. He didn't budge.

"Goddamn it. You'd better not be dead." Sean checked Mateo's pulse. It was steady. He dropped his head to the steering wheel. "You've got to be kidding me. Okay. Whatever." Sean started the car, talking to himself the way he tended to do. "It's cool. I totally wanted to drag a man twice my size from my car to my couch. It's not like I didn't spend the last seventeen hours on my feet. No biggie." Sean snorted. "Rapist." With his fit at an end, Sean did what he always did: he let it go. At least he wasn't alone. He couldn't remember the last time that happened.

2

The room was a pale yellow. Mateo didn't have a single room in his house painted that color. It was also bright. Mateo liked to party on the weekends and always kept his curtains drawn tight. He rolled. His arms and legs scrambled for purchase as he met nothing but empty air. Luckily, it wasn't that far of a drop from the unfamiliar couch to the floor. Unfortunately, he landed on hardwood flooring. He blinked at the ceiling and tried gathering his bearings. A face appeared over him.

"You're alive."

Those sexy green eyes. That sweet smile. "Sean?"

"You're alive and you remember my name," he said as he bent to lend Mateo a hand up.

Mateo accepted, because even after trying to kill

himself with alcohol, he still wanted to touch the sexy waiter, but he didn't let the man bear the brunt of his weight. Mateo was solid muscle. He was too conscious of hurting the slim and sexy man who'd rescued him from the parking lot of Slip. It was all coming back to him. He'd been plastered and couldn't remember where he'd left his Jeep.

"You brought me to your house? I might've been a serial killer or a rapist." Mateo thought it over before adding, "Or both. A serial rapist."

Sean's sexy smile didn't abate. "So you said last night."

Mateo's brows drew together. "Did I?"

A gorgeous laugh filled the air. Even feeling like death, with the world's worst headache and cottonmouth, Mateo recognized he'd never heard a sexier sound. "Yes. Would you like some coffee?"

Mateo couldn't let it go. "You could've gotten hurt. For real, Sean."

Something dark passed over Sean's features before quickly disappearing. "I didn't. There's some pain relievers on the table and I made a quiche."

"You made quiche?" Mateo heard himself. He hadn't been awake even five minutes and his brain wasn't functioning. "Like from scratch? On a Saturday morning?" Mateo couldn't stop. He didn't know what time it was, but didn't normal people sleep in, and not make food for strangers who could've killed them in their sleep?

Sean's smile fell. He twisted his fingers and Mateo immediately felt like shit. The man had been nothing but nice and good. Mateo had been nothing but a dick. "It's sort of my thing," Sean said, sounding unsure. "I'm in my final year at Monsieur Julliam's Culinary School."

Mateo searched his fogged brain. He'd heard the name. It clicked. "Isn't that place impossible to get into?"

Sean's smile was back. He nodded. "Food is my passion." He headed for the kitchen and Mateo followed because that ass. He couldn't look away. A small glass-topped kitchen table came into view. Sure enough, there was a quiche and coffee. Jesus, this man might be the love of his life. It smelled freaking amazing. No wonder he'd been pulled from an alcohol-fueled sleep of the dead.

"Whoa. This looks delicious."

"Thanks," Sean said, blushing. He motioned toward an empty chair. "Please, sit. I'll grab you a plate and mug." It seemed wrong for Mateo to let Sean wait on him inside the man's house, but he sat. Sean returned with a plate, silverware, and coffee mug. He filled the cup before motioning toward a small turntable at the edge of the table. "There's creamer and sugar over there, if you need it."

Mateo winked, hoping his head wouldn't explode as he lifted the mug to his lips. It was black all the way for him. He didn't need the extra calories and the hangover threatening to kill him demanded something strong. Sean claimed the seat across from him and doctored his cup while Mateo let the bubbling hot liquid scald him awake.

"I'm glad you didn't die," Sean said after a moment.

Mateo's eyebrows rose. "Was that a fear?"

Sean nodded. "I've called a lot of cabs for a lot of wasted customers, but I've never seen one as bad off as you were."

Sean's words gave away more than Mateo thought he intended. The man didn't bring home strangers, even while saving them. Mateo was unique in some way. "Why didn't you call me a cab?"

Instead of answering, Sean nodded toward Mateo's cup. "Is the coffee okay? I make it a little strong for some people."

"It's perfect." Mateo couldn't stop staring at Sean as he made the claim. To keep from making an ass of himself, especially since he didn't doubt for a second he'd done that last night, Mateo took a bite of his food. Holy hell. It practically melted on his tongue. "Jesus. This is amazing, baby." The endearment rolled off

Mateo's tongue without thought. It was mostly a habit. He grew up in a household where everyone was "baby." Sean beamed. Mateo blew out an inner sigh of relief. Honest to God, he didn't know how to act. Everything about the situation was more awkward than sneaking away after sex with a stranger. Sean couldn't have been a nicer guy if he tried. The word "nice" was practically stamped on the dude's forehead. The man had rescued a drunk stranger who could've killed him and it was obvious he didn't regret it. Mateo's discomfort slipped away. Honestly, that was the kind of crazy Mateo could get behind. This guy was great.

SEAN HAD to practically threaten to break Mateo's fingers to stop him from doing the dishes before they left the apartment. Despite the threat, Sean kept forcing his smile away. Maybe Mateo was a player, as his friend claimed, but he also had manners and worried over Sean taking home a stranger. There was a good guy in there. Sean didn't think he'd have to dig deep to find him.

They pulled into Slip's parking lot. Even though they weren't set to open for a few more hours, there were at least five cars in the lot. It seemed Mateo wasn't the only one who hadn't been fit to drive home last night. "Which car is yours?"

Mateo motioned toward a black Jeep Wrangler Unlimited. "That one."

Of course. It looked like Mateo's car. Sean drove through the lot and parked next to the driver's side. "Here you go. Driver's side service."

Mateo didn't budge. "Let me see your phone."

"For?"

The dimples were back. "I'm want to program my number in your phone. That way the ball is in your court if you want to see me again."

Sean shook his head and dug out his phone. He handed it over. Mateo turned it over in his hands. The screen was cracked and the edges were scratched, but it still worked. Sean wasn't the type to waste money on buying new things unless he had no other choice. "It's seen some stuff," Sean explained.

Mateo chuckled. Sean had to take a deep breath to fortify himself against the sound. "That's putting it mildly. If it gets the job done, though," Mateo said as he typed in his number.

"Seventy-five percent of the time," Sean admitted, uncaring what Mateo thought. Everything he had, he'd worked for.

Mateo handed the phone back. "There. Now you can cyber stalk me."

"It's like a fairy tale ending," Sean said, fighting the urge to find something else for them to do and dragging out their time together.

With a wink, Mateo opened the door. "Except it's not the end. You'll call."

Sean's cheeks ached. "I will?"

"Yep," Mateo said, sounding confident. "You've already seen me drunk. That's like fourth date material. Thank you for everything," Mateo added before Sean could think of something witty to say.

The sincerity in Mateo's tone pulled at Sean's heartstrings. "You're welcome. If I don't call, it's been great meeting you."

"You too, but you'll call," Mateo said as he closed the door, stopping Sean from arguing. Sean glanced at his phone. It was open to his text messages, and he'd already sent one to Mateo. Sean snorted out a laugh. He texted him again.

Sean: *Did you text yourself so you could save my number?*

Mateo pulled his phone from his back pocket as he climbed in his Jeep. A half second passed.

Mateo: *Yep.*

Sean: *I thought you said the ball was in my court.*

Mateo: *It was, and you texted me first. Now the ball's in mine.*

Shaking his head, Sean glanced over, wishing

Mateo's windows weren't tinted so dark he couldn't see him. He was torn—part of him wanted to see the man's face while another part of him wanted to flip Mateo off. All of Sean hoped they'd see each other again.

———

THE ONLY THING that saved Sean's pride was that Mateo texted him first. Well, that, and no one was there to witness his reaction to Mateo's name finally appearing on the face of his phone. He might have done a happy dance. No one would ever know.

Mateo: *Come see me.*

Sean: *I have 2 hours between school and work. I need to eat and then crash for a few because I'm SO exhausted.*

Mateo: *Let me take care of you. I'll send you my address, have food waiting, and then I promise you can sleep.*

Sean: *Okay.*

He wasn't prepared, but seriously, there was no way he could've braced himself. Mateo's house was huge. Sean should've expected as much when Mateo sent him a code to get through the front gate. Stupidly, Sean had thought Mateo possibly lived in one of the upper scale apartment complexes. Both those places had gates. Nope. Seeing Mateo's home almost sent Sean running for the hills. The place cost a couple million easy. Sean couldn't think straight, much less breathe properly. What had he gotten himself into?

From where he parked, Sean could see the brick boat dock and boat sitting on the water where Sean's home had direct access to the ocean. The beige stone house was three stories high and everything about it gleamed. As he moved closer to the side door Mateo had directed him to, Sean spotted an L-shaped pool looking over the edge of the water. He wanted to die right then. Instead, he opened the arched door Mateo said would be unlocked for him. The scent of apples and cinnamon wafted over him as soon as the cool indoor air hit his skin. Of course the place smelled like freaking heaven. Spotting a pile of shoes by the door in what appeared to be a mud room, Sean toed off his shoes and left them behind. The instant he stepped through the doorway and into the kitchen, Mateo appeared. Everything else disappeared. His sexy smile held Sean captivated.

"You came."

Sean smiled at the surprise in Mateo's tone. "I said I would."

Mateo shifted, looking uncomfortable. "Still, I wasn't sure."

He was so sexy. The way Mateo's white T-shirt stretched across his cut body had nothing to do with it.

Sean couldn't explain what it was about Mateo. It was in his eyes. "Do you get stood up often?"

Something dark passed over Mateo's features, fascinating Sean. "You'd be surprised." Sean doubted anyone ever turned this down. "Anyhow," Mateo said before Sean could voice his doubts, "I have zucchini lasagna. It sounds disgusting, but I promise it's not."

A smile tugged at Sean's lips. "Actually, that sounds delicious. I'm starving."

Mateo motioned toward an open doorway. From where they stood, Sean could see a large dining room table. The food waiting for them didn't hold his attention anywhere near as much as the gorgeous view of palm trees and water through the window. "I kept everything warm."

Sean's feet moved even as his gaze remained locked on the window. "Your house is beautiful. I had no idea boxing paid so well. If I had, I wouldn't have taken so many free ass kickings over the years."

A bark of laughter escaped Mateo as if Sean's words surprised him. "Some boxers make huge piles of money. I'm not one of them. All of this is thanks to being my grandmother's favorite." He held out a chair for Sean before claiming the empty seat next to him. "When she died, she left everything to me, because— for one—my parents didn't need the money, and two, she knew I'd be homeless otherwise."

Sean took a bite and swallowed. He pointed at his dish. "That's delicious. Why would you have been homeless?"

Mateo sipped his wine before responding. "It's takeout. Sorry I didn't ask what you'd like. I'm a bit of a health nut."

Sean smiled at Mateo's obvious avoidance of the topic. "That's fine. I told you food is my passion. I love all of it. You didn't answer my question." Mateo took a huge bite as if he didn't intend to cooperate. Sean kept staring at him, leaving him no choice. "I don't have all day," Sean reminded him.

Mateo snorted. "Fine. My dad is a very successful acquisitionist. The richest of the rich pay him to procure things for them—like exotic cars and other items that are difficult to acquire or import. They like having nice things but don't like working to find them, so my dad does the work."

"I assume this is an extremely well-paying job."

Mateo nodded. "But don't let that fact fool you into thinking I'm spoiled." Sean took another bite to stop himself from pointing out their current surroundings. Luckily, Mateo kept talking. "He's big on working for what you want. If anything, despite my parents' wealth, I had to work twice as hard for everything. Most kids got the latest gaming systems for Christmas. I had to mow lawns for two summers. That sort of thing. I'd already been informed that when I turned eighteen, I'd have to get out and make my own way. It didn't matter I wouldn't graduate high school for four months afterward. My grandmother let me come live with her. I worked just as hard for her, but unlike my parents, she tended to spoil me. When I told her I wanted to box professionally, she was all for it. She died when I was twenty-one."

By the time Mateo finished his story, Sean had cleaned his plate and was polishing off the wine. He loved listening to Mateo talk. His accent wasn't thick, but it was hot. Occasionally, he slightly rolled an R. Sean kind of wanted to feel it against his tongue. He straightened in his seat at the thought and pulled his mind back on track. "How did your parents handle her leaving you everything?"

A bitter-looking smile touched Mateo's lips. "Not well. In truth, if she hadn't ensured her will was ironclad, I'm certain they would've fought me in court even though they don't need the money."

"That's sad."

"You're tired," Mateo reminded him, as if hoping Sean would let the subject drop. He did. After all, his past wasn't one he wanted Mateo digging around in. He should give the man the same courtesy. "Exhausted," Sean clarified. "I don't think I've had a solid eight hours of sleep in years."

"You should take the night off and let me spoil you," Mateo said, lifting his glass to his lips.

Sean bit back a sigh of longing at the thought. "Boston and Kaz—those are my bosses," he explained. "They've been really good to me. I can't leave them shorthanded on such short notice." There. That sounded better than admitting he couldn't afford to miss a single second of work.

"I actually know Boston well."

Sean blinked. "Really?"

Mateo nodded. "He used to be Middleweight champion."

"Oh," Sean said, feeling a bit stupid. "Seems like I remember hearing something like that. Sorry. I don't keep up with sports."

Mateo's smile had Sean's stomach growling like he hadn't just eaten. "Stop apologizing. I'm surprised you have time for anything." He came to his feet. "Since you've squeezed me in, I'll spend what little time you can spare for me, doing what you need—sleeping. Let's go."

Skepticism set in even as Sean stood. "We really are sleeping, right?"

Mateo flashed a wicked smile over his shoulder. "Trust me."

Maybe he was stupid, but Sean did trust Mateo. After all, the man had slept under Sean's roof and hadn't killed him in his sleep. This was a small thing by comparison. "Okay," Sean said as he accepted Mateo's hand and let the man lead him down the hall. He caught glimpses of each room they passed. Despite not getting a good look, Sean was still impressed by how gorgeous everything was. There was so much polished wood and leather. He almost tripped over his feet when they passed a home gym. "Why do you go to the gym every day if you have one already?"

"I don't have a trainer here."

"Oh," Sean said, still trying to keep up. When they reached the end of the hall, Mateo led Sean inside a huge bedroom. He knew immediately it was Mateo's space by the smell alone. It was like squishing his face in one of Mateo's shirts and inhaling his cologne. Sean fought the urge to close his eyes and breathe it in. Despite the size of the room, it still seemed like the man's bed took up too much space. It was set up high and looked squishy. The comforter was balled up in the center of the bed.

"Don't worry. I know it looks a mess, but that's because I never make my bed. There's a woman who comes in and cleans once a week. She was just here two days ago, and she always changes the bedding."

Sean hadn't even thought of cleanliness. His brain never moved past a woman coming in to clean. "I'm not worried."

Mateo motioned toward the bed. "I sleep in the middle, so feel free to pick a side."

Sean circled the bed and climbed in. "Holy shit," Sean breathed as the mattress shifted with him, molding to his skin. "Okay, I'm officially in love with this mattress." He rolled to his side and fluffed up the pillow, more than ready to let the amazing bed carry him away.

The bed didn't even move at his side as Mateo climbed in. That was why it surprised him when Mateo's arm draped over him. "Is this okay?"

Sean took stock of the situation at Mateo's question. The man's breath brushed over his neck every time he exhaled and his hard chest pressed against Sean's shoulder blades, but the lower half of his body didn't touch Sean. "Yeah. I'm good." It was true. Mateo showed him more respect and kindness than anyone ever had. It was refreshing and made Sean's chest feel heavy with some unnamed emotion. Still, he was certain there was no way he'd fall asleep with Mateo's heavy arm pinning him to the bed. That was the last thought Sean had before a beeping noise had his eyes flying open. He searched the room with his gaze. Mateo's phone was lit up on the bed, making a god-awful noise. Mateo slept on like a dead man. The screen flashed "stop" so Sean tapped it. The phone fell silent. He checked the time. Two hours had gone by in an instant. Sean still couldn't believe he'd fallen asleep so quickly.

Rolling over, he stared at Mateo's sleeping form. In his sleep, the man looked five years younger, which reminded him he'd never asked Mateo how old he was. He should do that. Sean wanted to know everything about the man sleeping next to him. There was a scar under his eye. Sean imagined it probably came from some fight, but he didn't know and wanted to. He blew out a slow breath. As much as he wanted to stay there all night, Sean had to get moving. Being with Mateo wasn't reality. Reality was working his ass off for little to no reward. Maybe Mateo would call him again. Chances were good he wouldn't, since Sean had more than proved he didn't put out. Either way, Sean would never forget Mateo's kindness. The man gave Sean something he was certain Mateo hadn't realized he'd given—hope.

MATEO BLINKED INTO THE DARKNESS, trying to remember where he was. He'd fallen asleep next to Sean, but he'd set his alarm for six. Mateo's gaze shot to the spot where Sean had been. The bed was empty.

"Fuck."

He checked his phone. It was eight twenty, and

he'd missed two calls. They were both from his mom. He cleared his call history. Why hadn't Sean woken him before leaving? Mateo rolled, trying to gather his bearings. After blinking a few times, the fog coating his mind cleared. He couldn't remember the last time he'd fallen asleep so fast and slept so hard. After scrubbing his hand over his face, he pushed to his feet and headed for the bathroom. Damn, he hated not getting to tell Sean goodbye. The man didn't have many free hours in the day. Mateo wanted them for himself. One hot shower later, Mateo knew what he had to do. Sean struck him as the type to melt away if Mateo let him. That was unacceptable. Mateo had the man in his sights now.

Thankfully, Slip was dead. There were only a few cars in the parking lot and one of those was Sean's. The hostess smiled as he came through the door. "Hi. How are you tonight? You have your pick of tables," she said, obviously running down some script rather than caring how he was doing. That was fine. Mateo didn't care to chat.

"Any place in Sean's section is good with me."

She grabbed a menu. "Great choice. Sean is awesome."

"He is," Mateo agreed, following on her heels to a table in the corner.

She set the menu on the table. "I'll let him know you're waiting."

Mateo nodded and sat. He didn't watch her go. Instead, he chose to look over the menu as if he hadn't been there a hundred times before. A shadow fell over him. Mateo glanced up and into the face of an angel. His mind went blank the way it always did when he saw Sean. "You didn't say goodbye." Even he didn't know why those were the first words from his mouth when his brain screamed so many other things.

The bravery that Sean had shown when they met appeared, fanning the flames of Mateo's interest. "You looked really sexy sleeping next to me. I didn't have the heart to wake you."

Mateo sat forward in his seat. He was a confident person by nature, but Sean stroked his ego like no one else had in years. "We should do something when you get off."

A flash of disappointment crossed Sean's features. "I have to close tonight and then be up at five a.m. to head to school." He winced. "I'm sorry. My days are pretty stretched for time."

It was obvious Sean wasn't trying to blow him off. His life was full. Mateo didn't want to make the man's life harder, but he wasn't giving up. "So come see me again between school and work. I'll keep you fed and well-rested."

Sean pulled a face. "Even though that sounds like heaven to me, that'll get old for you pretty quick."

Mateo snorted. "Are you joking? Eating and sleeping are two of my top ten favorite things to do. Plus, you get nights off, right?"

Sean nodded.

Mateo beamed. "See? I won't get left out. Come see me tomorrow."

Even though Sean still didn't look convinced, he gave in. "Okay. But," he added, stealing the fire from Mateo's triumph. "If you get sick of me, you have to tell me. I mean it."

"You got it," Mateo said, knowing it wouldn't happen. "Now pick me out something good to eat. I'm sick of always eating the same things."

The smile stretching Sean's lips bordered on evil. "You should never say that to a chef. Well, chef-in-training."

Somehow, Mateo managed to lean even closer to Sean. It still wasn't close enough. "Blow my mind," he said, daring Sean with his tone and stare.

"Don't worry. I will."

Mateo no longer knew if they were talking about food. It didn't matter. Sean had already wowed him in a dozen ways. Everything from this moment on was just icing.

3

*D*amn, Mateo hated when Sean left without saying goodbye. Two days in a row it had happened. Since he'd done it only three days out of the past month, Mateo tried letting it slide. Rolling to his side, Mateo snagged Sean's pillow and held it to his chest. Sean's scent lingered on the material. His eyes fell closed as he inhaled the sweet smell into his lungs. Mateo's dick stirred. He tossed the pillow aside and grabbed his phone. He couldn't let it slide after all.

Mateo: *You left without saying goodbye again.*

Sean: *I can't help it. You were sleeping so peacefully. I couldn't bring myself to wake you.*

Mateo: *I'd rather see you than sleep. **sigh** I take it you made it safely.*

Sean: *Yeah. I had another flat, but thankfully I just got that other tire fixed and the spare was in the trunk again.*

Mateo wanted to break shit. Sean had the worst luck. He wanted to fix everything in Sean's life, but the man had more pride than anyone he'd ever met.

Mateo: *You should've called.*

Sean: *I took care of it. No worries.*

Mateo: *Yeah, yeah. I know you're capable. That doesn't mean I won't worry.*

Sean: *Your concern matters.*

Mateo: *You matter.*

Sean: *Has anyone told you lately how amazing you are?*

Mateo: *Not that I can recall.*

Sean: *Yeah, I'm sure. You probably have ten men telling you you're perfect every day.*

He didn't. What Mateo really had was two parents who took turns telling him he was a piece of shit and a bunch of non-friends who made him feel like he had to hide behind a mask. Sean was the only person who let him be boring and still came back for more. Mateo stared at the phone, trying to decide what to say. Another text rolled in before he could think of something.

Sean: *I'll be number 11. You're so freaking amazing. It's probably your picture showing under the definition of fantastic. I bet sonnets have been written in your name. A* *thousand stars have fallen from the sky with wishes to be with you. How was that?*

Mateo snorted. "Sonnets." Even as he laughed, his chest ached. He took a deep breath. It sounded ragged in the silence of his bedroom.

Mateo: *That was perfect. Have a good night at work, baby.*

Sean: *Have a good night at the gym. I'll see you tomorrow.*

Mateo: *See ya.*

Mateo stared at the phone for longer than he cared to admit, reading over all their texts. There was so much written between the lines of every text they'd sent in the past month. He wanted to give Sean the world. Even if they were never more than they were right now, he was better for having met Sean. Mateo wanted Sean to feel like his life was better for having him as well.

Mateo stared at the ceiling. He held the phone to his chest as if it brought Sean closer. When they'd crawled into bed earlier, Mateo had taken up his usual position at Sean's back. Sean had scooted back, pressing closer to Mateo than usual. Mateo had pushed a step further as well, by shoving his hand beneath Sean's shirt, holding him skin on skin. It had taken him twice as long to fall asleep. He'd been walking around with blue balls for so long now, he was surprised he hadn't started snapping off people's heads.

Mateo rolled, letting his feet hit the floor. He stared down at his bare feet. This house felt so goddamn empty without Sean, and he was only there two hours out of the day and a few hours on his nights off. Mateo couldn't stop himself; he sent off another text.

Mateo: *I miss you. How can I make your life easier?*

Sean: *Miss you too. Do something to make yourself happy today. That would make me smile.*

That wasn't what he'd asked, but Mateo recognized it was all he'd get. A smile exploded across Mateo's face. He knew exactly what would make him happy, and Sean had told him to do it.

EVERYTHING HURT, and he was dying. Sean needed just two days off in a row. It didn't sound like much to ask, but he hadn't had two back-to-back days off in probably a year. He suppressed a yawn as he circled his car, making sure his spare tire had made it through the night, especially since this was the third time this month he'd had to use it.

Sean stood blinking at his tires. He circled the car once more, trying to grasp what he was seeing. All four tires were new. He unlocked the driver's side door gingerly, half expecting his key wouldn't work, and it wasn't his car. It opened easily. Sean slid behind the wheel. For several minutes, he stared into space— thinking. Only one person would've done such a thing. Sean couldn't decide if he was angry. He wanted to be. Mateo was already more of everything than Sean. Sean didn't want to be a charity case or a project. The moment the balance of power swung Mateo's way, Sean would come out the loser.

He put the car in reverse. Sleep was overrated. Instead of turning left and heading for his apartment, Sean turned right. When he reached Mateo's house, the place was dark and Sean second guessed himself. What if Mateo wasn't alone? They weren't in a relationship and Sean hadn't called ahead. Mateo might be in bed with someone else. They might be in Sean's spot or beneath Mateo's hard body. Sean's stomach twisted in a knot. He turned the car off but didn't move. Torn didn't even begin to describe what he felt. Mateo wasn't his. He felt like his. Why had he come here again? Did his pride matter as much as his heart? Because he didn't doubt for a second it would break him to see Mateo with someone else. Mateo's friend had said Mateo would fuck anything that moved. If it was true, then it stood to reason Mateo had slept with other people since meeting him.

Sean fought the urge to hyperventilate. In the

grand scheme of things, did tires matter enough to chance getting hurt? The driver's side door opened. Mateo's hand appeared in front of his face—palm up. Sean followed the line of Mateo's arm to the man's face. His expression gave nothing away. Sean accepted Mateo's outstretched hand.

Mateo tugged. "Come on, baby. You're exhausted."

Sean let Mateo lead him inside. "How did you know I was here?"

Mateo's arm encircled Sean's waist, as if steadying him. The gesture made Sean wonder if he looked as bad as he felt. "I've been keeping an eye out for you. I knew your rage would bring you my way."

"Teo, I feel really bad. Maybe I should go home."

"Nope," Mateo said, sweeping Sean into his arms.

"I don't want to be out of balance," Sean said, only mildly curious as to why his words were slurred and he couldn't walk. "You take care of me every day and buy me new tires. Now I'm fucking sick. It's not fair." Sean was beyond caring if he sounded childish. "I want to be the one making your life better."

Mateo wore a huge grin as he set Sean on the bed, pulled his socks and shoes off, and covered him with the comforter. "Baby, you have no idea how much you give me by just being here and saying things like that. Now, are you off tomorrow or do I need to call Boston?"

"I'm off."

"Good," Mateo said as he moved to switch off the lights.

As always, the mattress didn't even budge as Mateo slid in next to Sean and gathered him in his arms. Sean couldn't fight. His strength was zapped, but he could argue. "No. I don't want to get you sick."

Mateo's lips touched his forehead. "Shush, baby. I'm trying to sleep."

Despite the fact that Sean was certain he was dying, he still smiled. "Teo."

"Yeah?"

"Thank you."

Mateo's lips brushed Sean's forehead again. This time, they lingered. "There's nothing I wouldn't do for you."

"I was scared to come inside." Fuck. He must be feverish. Sean couldn't stop telling on himself.

"Why? You know you're always welcome here."

He swallowed. His throat hurt. "I didn't know if you'd be with someone else." Sean didn't get specific. The vulnerability in his tone said more than he'd ever meant to say.

"There's no one else."

"Oh," Sean said for lack of anything more. His eyes slid closed. He was freezing and Mateo was so warm.

"Sean."

Sean couldn't pry his eyes open. "Yeah?"

"Don't think that again, okay?"

"Okay," Sean said, incapable of speaking above a whisper. He trusted Mateo. If the man said he shouldn't think bad thoughts, he wouldn't.

"Go to sleep, baby. I'll make you better."

Sean knew he would. Mateo always made everything better.

SEAN: *I'm bringing dinner tonight. You shouldn't have to feed us every time.*

Mateo: *I like feeding you.*

Sean: *It's my turn.*

SEAN: *Do you ever eat sweets?*

Mateo: *Are you joking? I love pie.*

Sean: *Only pie? What about cake?*

Mateo: *Yum. Cake.*

Sean: *We made cakes today in class. I'm bringing some with me tonight.*

Mateo: *Hell yeah!*

MATEO: *When is your next night off?*

    Sean: *Friday.*

    Mateo: *There's a movie I want to see. Can we go?*

    Sean: *Whatever makes you happy.*

    Mateo: *I like the sound of that.*

MATEO: *I'll be in NOLA this weekend for a fight.*

    Sean: *Okay.*

    Mateo: *I'll miss you.*

    Sean: *I'll miss you too, but I wouldn't have gotten to see you much anyhow. I have to work all weekend.*

    Mateo: *Still. Maybe we can FaceTime when you get off? **hopeful face***

    Sean: *I'd love that.*

THE SIGHT of a sexy caramel-skinned man sitting in his section was something Sean needed more than oxygen. A smile stretched his lips and his feet moved faster than he intended. "Hey." Even to Sean's ears, he sounded breathless.

Gah, the dimples. Sean couldn't take it. "Hey, baby."

Sean fought the urge to steal a kiss. His reaction startled even him, but his palms itched from the need to touch Mateo. "I thought you were headed to the gym."

Mateo nodded. "In a minute. I needed to ask you something, and I didn't want to get you in trouble by not buying something while I'm here."

"You could've texted me," Sean reminded him.

With a shake of his head, Mateo dismissed Sean's words. "Not if I wanted to see you too."

Sean bit his bottom lip to keep from smiling like an idiot. "Then I'm glad you felt you needed to ask in person."

"Damn, happy looks so fucking sexy on you," Mateo said as if the words were meant more for himself. He shook his head as if shaking off a trance. Happiness roared through Sean. Mateo was right. His whole body radiated with joy. Thankfully, Mateo kept talking and stopped Sean from climbing on a table to announce his secret longing. He was an idiot over Mateo. "If I gave you a ticket to my match in New Orleans, do you think there's any way you could come?"

Mateo's question brought Sean back to reality. He wanted to say yes. Mateo never asked him for anything. It was like a dagger through his heart to say no. "It's this Friday, right?"

"Yes." Mateo looked crestfallen, as if he already knew Sean would turn him down.

Sean wanted to scream at the top of his lungs at how unfair life was. He didn't want to hurt Mateo. He tried letting him down easy. "Mateo, it's not that I don't want to go. I can't afford to go to New Orleans. Boston might let me take the time off, but I'm poor. I'd have to save two years at this point to get five miles north of Miami."

"Oh, okay. I shouldn't have put you in this position by asking."

Goddamn it. Mateo looked defeated, and it was twisting the knife in Sean's heart. After casting a quick look around and not seeing his boss, Sean pulled out a chair and sat. "Sweetie, you know I'd drop everything and be there in a heartbeat if I could. There's just no way. I'm barely scraping by. My light bill is already two days late. Everything I own is on its last leg. If there was any way at all, I would be there."

Mateo's eyes lit. Sean got a bad feeling he'd been maneuvered. "Come with me. I've already got the room and a ticket to the match. It wouldn't cost you anything but your time."

"And a plane ticket," Sean grumbled, because he had a strong suspicion he'd be headed to a fight on Friday.

Mateo shook his head. "You're coming to support me. Let me take care of that."

"What about your parents?" If roles were reversed, Sean's parents would want to be there. He didn't want to steal a ticket from them.

A heartbreaking smile touched Mateo's lips before falling away. "They won't be there. My dad says I'm a gatekeeper and always will be, so there's no sense in him wasting his time and money to watch me lose."

"What's a gatekeeper?" Sean had no idea how his question came out sounding so calm. He really wanted to set fire to something, preferably something Mateo's dad loved.

"Basically, I'm the guy everyone else has to beat to get to the titleholder, but I'm no real challenge to the boxer who currently holds the title."

Sean ground his back teeth and swallowed hard, trying to keep his opinions to himself. No good could come of him saying a damn thing. A burst of laughter escaped Mateo. "I wish you could see your face. It's killing you to keep silent."

"Maybe," Sean said, sounding childish and not caring.

"If I thought you'd let me, I'd kiss you right now."

The confession had Sean's anger melting away and his nerves set in. If Mateo kissed him, Sean would let him. He couldn't believe Mateo hadn't realized that by now. "You need to get to the gym," he said to stop himself from begging for that kiss.

Mateo sighed. It sounded resigned. "If I must." His mouth lifted in one corner and one gorgeous dimple made an appearance. Sean knew whatever came out of Mateo's mouth next would probably get Sean in trouble. "Come with me to New Orleans," he begged, proving Sean's suspicions right.

Heat flared in Sean's face at the wickedness in Mateo's expression. "Let me talk to Boston."

Mateo's gaze never wavered from Sean's. "You should definitely come with me."

Sean huffed. "You won't let this go, will you?"

"Mateo, you're always here, distracting my best server," Boston said, appearing out of nowhere and squeezing Mateo's shoulder. Judging by Mateo's wince, the gesture wasn't as friendly as Boston's tone.

"I disagree," Mateo said, matching Boston's bright tone. "Your restaurant is distracting my man from giving me all his attention."

Sean's gaze slid to Boston's. That was the safe place to look. Mateo was always saying things like that, and Sean didn't know where to go with it.

Boston winked, letting Sean know he wasn't as upset as he pretended to be with Mateo. "You should be at the gym, training for your match."

"I'll go as soon as you agree to let Sean off this weekend so he can go with me."

Sean wanted to hide his face.

Boston didn't hesitate. "Done. Get out."

Mateo came to his feet. Sean followed. "Wow. What a way to treat a paying customer," Mateo said, laughing.

"Jesus," Boston muttered. He met Sean's gaze. "Walk your man to his car and get him out of here but be quick about it."

Sean barely suppressed a happy burst of laughter. He was too happy to try correcting Boston's assumption. Nonetheless, Sean made a silent promise to himself that he'd work himself into the ground for Boston when he got back. The man deserved a trophy for putting up with Sean.

THE TRIP to New Orleans had to be quick since Mateo knew Sean really couldn't afford to be off work like this. He still couldn't believe he'd convinced Sean to go. He was so thankful. It sucked ass not having a single person cheering for him. As always, he'd invited his parents, and they'd refused. He'd gone straight to Sean's work afterward and threw himself on the man's mercy. It had been a dirty move, but Mateo had no one else. He'd won his fight easily, knowing Sean was watching. In fact, it had only lasted three rounds.

There wasn't as much after-event stuff to take care of, since it wasn't a title match. Media didn't pay much attention to the little guys. This was one time Mateo was thankful for it. They had an early flight back home in the morning, but they still had a few hours to enjoy the nightlife.

"I'm sorry this wasn't more of a vacation for you," Mateo said, happily holding Sean's hand as they walked down Decatur Street.

"Are you kidding me? I've never been here. This is more than I expected."

Mateo swallowed down his hatred for how hard Sean's life was. The man took it in stride. Mateo didn't want to. "You should let me take you somewhere for a full week. If anyone deserves a real vacation, it's you."

A sexy-sounding chuckle escaped Sean. "We live in one of the most beautiful places in the world. I don't need to go elsewhere."

Mateo's growl was out of his control. "It drives me insane you won't let me do anything for you."

Sean squeezed his hand, pulling Mateo's focus his way. Mateo was surprised by how serious Sean looked. "You do a lot for me. Every single day. For once, why don't you tell me what I can do for you?"

"You're doing it," Mateo said with a shrug. He looked away. "No one else spends time with me."

"Then everyone you know is stupid," Sean said, sounding like an over-protective parent and pulling a laugh from Mateo.

Mateo fell silent as they turned right and headed for the water's edge. Warm night air blew in from the river, tousling Sean's hair. Mateo automatically pushed it behind Sean's ear. He'd never met anyone who made him want to take care of them the way Sean did. The man was like a puppy in a world of wolves.

"What are you thinking about?" Sean asked, making Mateo realize he'd been standing there, staring at Sean in silence for longer than necessary.

"Why aren't you married or something equally tied down? Is everyone you know stupid too? Because I know you, and there's nothing wrong with you."

A sad smile touched Sean's lips. "You'd be surprised."

Mateo couldn't resist pushing Sean's hair behind his ear again. He looked so damn gorgeous with the river and night sky behind him. Mateo searched for every excuse to touch him. "Every time I ask a question about your life, you look sad."

"I'm not sad," Sean said in a quiet voice. His gaze never wavered from Mateo's. "In fact, I've never been happier than I am right now."

"Me too," Mateo heard himself admit. "Really, it's been that way since meeting you."

Sean reached out and cupped Mateo's face between his hands, stealing Mateo's breath. The man's touch was light, but it paralyzed Mateo. "I don't like watching you get hit," Sean said, his gaze moving over Mateo's face. "This split lip looks like it hurts."

Mateo's brain screamed for him to seize his chance and tell Sean how he felt. He'd never been more terrified. If he spoke up and lost Sean's friendship, he wouldn't have anyone in his life again. Mateo smiled, taking care not to smile so big it split his lip open again. "You should kiss it and make it better."

Mateo's body tensed as Sean's gaze dropped to his mouth. He held his breath. Sean took a step closer. Mateo could feel the heat radiating off Sean's body. He kept inching closer until Mateo could feel the man's breath brushing his skin. Mateo automatically lowered his head, making it easier for Sean to reach him. The space of a breath separated their lips. Mateo closed his eyes and silently begged for Sean's touch. He wondered if his body would fly apart as he waited.

Sean's lips brushed his so lightly Mateo barely felt it happen. As Sean leaned away, Mateo's body swayed toward him, needing more. Only by force of will alone did he stop himself.

"There," Sean said, moving out of reach. "We should find a club and get plastered."

"I like this plan," Mateo said, reclaiming Sean's hand. His heart needed medicine to numb its pain. It pined for Sean's love. In moments like this, he feared he'd never have it.

4

*S*ean: *I know it's Christmas time, but my family celebrates on Christmas Eve and I hoped you'd like to go with me. Also, they're having a work party at Slip to celebrate. I'd love it if you'd be my date.*

Mateo: *Only if you go with me to my parents on Christmas Day and to the training center for their holiday celebration thing.*

Sean: *I'm on school break and Slip is closing from Christmas Eve to January 2nd, so I have nothing but time.*

Mateo: *Awesome.*

The Slip party went off without a hitch. Boston had been thrilled to see Mateo. At least, as much as Boston was ever thrilled to see anyone. The man had charm, but Sean recognized most of it was faked. When Boston was with his husband, Kaz, he was someone else. They made Sean jealous sometimes because—in his heart—Sean knew he'd never have what they did.

Since Sean's work party turned out to be on the same day as the one at Mateo's training facility, they'd gone to Slip first. Mateo drove. Sean drank. He needed the fortification. Considering Sean worked with the public, meeting strangers shouldn't have been such a big deal, but the people who worked out with Mateo daily weren't strangers to Mateo. They'd be looking at Sean, judging, and finding him lacking. He spent the ride there talking himself off the ledge. Surely there'd be someone nice there, and not just the asshole who'd been at Slip with Mateo the night they'd met. He could do this. Mateo was with him. By the time they pulled in the parking lot of Aden's gym, he'd somewhat made peace with his current circumstances. The heated glances Mateo had been tossing his way all night definitely helped. They were such an odd mixture of friends and nothing at all. Yet, they weren't nothing. There was something there. Sean spent every moment in Mateo's company waiting for this thing between them to explode, destroying their friendship and turning messy. The good kind of messy. The kind that took over and controlled every thought.

Mateo ran around the Jeep and opened Sean's door, as if scared Sean would do it before he could get there —the way he always did. Sean let it go on because it was adorable. Mateo held his hand on the way to the door. He let go only long enough to hold the door open for Sean. Sean's steps faltered as he crossed the threshold. The place looked like the North Pole had exploded inside. It didn't snow in the Keys, but apparently it did inside Aden's gym.

The most beautiful man Sean had ever seen overcame him. Truly, it was like a gorgeous rocket launched at Sean's body. "Hiya. I'm Remy," the dude said as he hugged Sean like they weren't complete strangers. "And you're Sean," he added before Sean could speak. He grabbed Sean's hand and tugged, dragging Sean along in his wake. Sean cast a desperate look at Mateo. Judging by the man's huge smile, Mateo didn't intend to rescue him. "Don't worry about Mateo," Remy said over his shoulder. "He'll be along. Being as how he's always talking about you, he won't let me keep you but a minute, so we have to hurry."

Sean had no idea what was going on, but Remy said Mateo talked about him all the time. The knowledge had his cheeks aching from smiling. Several familiar faces stood out in the crowd as they passed. It seemed the men here frequented Slip. Finally, Remy's steps slowed as they reached the doorway of an office. He grabbed Sean's shoulders, maneuvering him into a specific position in the entryway. Sean went along, because... he had no idea why, but he was a little scared to disobey.

"There," Remy said, sounding triumphant. "Stand right there and don't move."

Sean nodded, because what choice did he have? He got the feeling people didn't say no to Remy often, and when they did, they immediately changed their mind if his smile fell. Remy disappeared inside the office and reappeared seconds later, holding a bright red box. He held it out to Sean. "Mateo told me you were coming."

The tips of Sean's fingers were numb as he accepted the gift. "You bought me a present?" Sean was beyond stunned and moved. He didn't even know who this guy was, and was afraid if he did, he'd have to be jealous, because he'd never compare to this guy.

Remy nodded. "Of course. You're a guest in my house. Well, technically, it's a gym, but still, it's my husband's gym and you've never been here."

Thank God. He was married. "I didn't bring you anything. Now I feel rude."

Remy waved off his words. "You brought me you. I've been super excited to meet you, but I don't go to Slip, so I've had to wait for you to come to me. Open your present." Remy was practically dancing in place.

Sean was hyper aware of Remy watching his every move as he lifted the lid on the box. There was an Aden's Gym T-shirt inside along with a generic holiday card. Sean scanned the front before flipping it open. "Welcome to the family. This card entitles you to one free year at Aden's Gym. Come hang out with your man and watch him in action on us. We'd love to know you better."

Sean glanced up—stunned. "Are you serious?"

Remy beamed. "Yes. Mateo is a huge part of our family here and we want you to be too. Trust me, having people who love and support you, surrounding you while you fight for a title—that's so, so important. One day soon, Mateo will win and he'll need you."

He didn't know what to say. Remy obviously believed Sean's relationship with Mateo was more than it was. He didn't have the heart to argue. Plus, he was moved. Sean didn't know how much a place like this cost per year, but even if it was a dollar, Sean couldn't afford it. He swallowed. "Thank you. This is one of the nicest things anyone has ever done for me."

Remy clapped and hugged him again. "Yay. We'll be such good friends. I just know it."

Mateo appeared from the crowd. "There you are." His gaze moved over Sean's face. No doubt, Sean looked every bit as emotional as he felt. "What did I miss?"

"Remy gave me a present." Sean's voice might've cracked on the last word. If so, he couldn't be held accountable.

"And he's standing under the mistletoe," Remy said, pointing at the plant hanging over Sean's head and sounding entirely too pleased with himself.

Mateo's gaze shifted to the spot above Sean's head before meeting Sean's stare once more. "So he is," he said, pushing the box Sean held aside before invading his space. Sean didn't have time to run or dodge. Mateo touched his chin, tilting Sean's head back, and claimed his mouth. He heard Remy giggle and then nothing else. Nothing could've prepared him. It wasn't innocent. This wasn't a game between friends. Mateo sucked Sean's bottom lip between his and lightly sank his teeth in. Sean couldn't move or react. Blood pounded in his ears and oxygen was nonexistent. Mateo teased Sean's mouth open with his tongue, and Sean let it happen. The stroke of Mateo's tongue against his was better than Sean imagined. He didn't want to stop. Reality waited at the end. Mateo was the first to pull away. He swiped the moisture from Sean's bottom lip with his thumb. Sean tried tearing his gaze away from Mateo's eyes, but there was something there. He wanted to beg for Mateo's thoughts.

Mateo looked away and focused on the box in Sean's hand. "What did you get?"

"Um." Sean glanced around. Remy was gone.

Without waiting for Sean to gather his thoughts,

Mateo sifted through the contents and read the card. "Whoa."

That shook Sean out his haze. "Was that an 'I can't believe you'll be hanging around all the time' whoa or a 'you don't want to know how much this gift is worth' whoa?"

"Definitely the second one." He set the card back in the box. "I'm thinking I owe Remy big time for giving me the gift of luring you here for the next year." He met Sean's gaze. "And for that kiss."

Sean couldn't breathe. "He seems great."

Mateo nodded. "Actually, he's the greatest person I've ever met. Well, he was, until I met you."

"I doubt I compare—"

Mateo kissed him again. This time, Sean didn't see it coming, but that didn't stop him from immediately opening for Mateo. It was quick—over as fast as it began.

"I think you should move out from underneath this mistletoe before someone else steals my place."

Sean stepped sideways and into the back of a man he hadn't noticed. The man turned. He had sweet-looking amber eyes and looked slightly familiar. "Excuse me," Sean muttered, moving away.

Amber Eyes smiled. "It's no problem. I'm Isaac," he said, holding out his hand for Sean to shake.

Sean shifted the box to the opposite arm and accepted. "Sean."

Isaac nodded. "I was at Slip with Mateo the night you two met."

Oh. That was where Sean had seen him. This wasn't the ass, but he'd still abandoned Mateo when he'd been drunk with no way home. Sean didn't know whether to kiss him or kick him. "I remember," he said instead.

Mateo took over. "Isaac is the Super Middleweight Champion."

"Seriously?" Sean asked, trying to sound impressed. Mostly, he was just uncomfortable. "I'm sorry. I don't keep up with sports."

Isaac shook his head. "Don't worry over it. I just won the title last week. Oh," he said, as if remembering something important. He turned slightly and drew the man he'd been speaking to, before Sean ran him down, forward. "This is Daniel."

He'd been there that night too. Sean remembered him. Still not the ass, so this was okay. Sean held out his hand. "Sean. Nice to meet you."

Daniel accepted and held on. "The pleasure's all mine. You should run."

A surprised snort of laughter escaped Sean. "What?"

Daniel kept shaking his hand. "Seriously. You

should run. Get as far away from this player as possible."

Sean realized he meant Mateo. A shot of anger roared through him. His face hardened. He felt it happen. "You should mind your own business."

Daniel dropped his hand and smiled as if nothing happened. "Can't. Sorry. I'm a reporter. Being nosy and intrusive is sort of my thing."

Sean's anger didn't abate. He recognized something in Daniel. Daniel was a controlling man. Sean hated those. It didn't matter if the man was the best person in every other way. Sean couldn't handle it. "If you need some info to make you feel better about this moment, I'm fine with that. Mateo is a damn good person. If you see me running, it's because I'm trying to get away from you." Sean turned away and caught sight of Mateo's stunned expression. He immediately felt like shit and turned back around. "I'm sorry," Sean said, not meeting Daniel's gaze. "You probably didn't deserve that."

The man's low chuckle had Sean's gaze sliding his way. Daniel was smiling. He looked younger and kinder. Sean's guilt tripled. "Actually, I completely deserved that. It was nice meeting you, Sean." Daniel and Isaac walked away, leaving Sean burning alive with embarrassment.

He cast an ashamed glance Mateo's way. "Jesus. I

completely understand if you never want to talk to me again, or—at least—don't want to be seen with me in public."

"Are you joking?" Mateo asked, sounding more serious than he'd ever heard the man. "You're my best friend. I don't know what I'd do if you never spoke to me again."

Sean's eyes burned. There was a real probability he might cry. No one had ever called him their best friend before. He didn't know what was happening between them. They felt like more than friends, but—raging hormones aside—Mateo was his best friend. His only friend. "That's probably the nicest thing anyone has ever said to me." Even as he made the claim, Sean expected Mateo would think he was pathetic.

"You're under the mistletoe again."

"It's okay if you want to kiss me again." In Sean's head, the words had rushed from his lips on a yell. In truth, they came out in a whisper that sounded closer to a plea. It seemed—when it came to Mateo—Sean didn't have any pride. Neither did he miss it.

———

MEETING SEAN'S parents had been nice. It turned out they were older, having started their family later in life. Sean's dad drove a fishing boat for party tours. Sean's mom altered clothes from their home. They weren't rich in money, but they were awesome. Neither parent had batted an eye over Mateo's presence. Mateo hadn't stopped smiling since Sean's mom had shyly admitted Sean had good taste.

Meeting Sean's parents was part one of Mateo's plans for the evening. They were headed to Mateo's parents' house first thing in the morning, and he'd yet to give Sean his gift. Mostly because he was nervous. "I've been thinking. You should stay the night at my house." He didn't give Sean time to argue. "It's late and we have to leave early."

No sound came from Sean's side of the car. Mateo chanced a glance. Sean was watching him. He wished he had time to inspect Sean's face and pick apart his mood, but he needed to watch the road. Sean finally responded. "Either way, we'll have to stop by my place. I need to get some clothes together and I don't have your gift with me."

A smile exploded across Mateo's face. "You bought me a gift?"

"Of course." Sean said the words as if it was a given, but Mateo knew how hard Sean struggled for everything.

"Guess we'd better run by your house, then," Mateo said, trying to keep the massive happiness from his voice.

"Give me five minutes," Sean said as he slid from the Jeep when they reached his apartment. "It won't take long for me to grab some clothes."

"Maybe grab more than one night's worth. You know, in case we're out late again tomorrow."

Sean smiled and shut the door. Mateo couldn't stop smiling as he watched Sean head inside. Staying true to his word, Mateo barely had time to miss him before he was back—overnight bag in hand.

"That was quick."

Sean winked. "I'm good."

"I'm sure," Mateo agreed as he backed out of his space. Damn, he wished Sean knew exactly how much Mateo would like to find out for himself. He hadn't stopped thinking about that kiss. Since meeting Sean almost three months ago, Mateo had fantasized more than he cared to admit. Remy had pointed out that mistletoe and Mateo had struck without thought. All he'd known was he didn't want to miss his chance. He'd thought to steal a small taste, but then he had Sean in his arms. Sean had kissed him back—like he'd been every bit as desperate. To make matters worse, Sean had immediately ripped into Daniel for him. No one ever stood up for him. Not only had Sean done so, he'd immediately apologized, because his heart was so goddamn pure. Mateo spent all his time torn right down the middle. Should he marry Sean before he wised up or send the man packing before he destroyed him?

"You're being awful quiet."

"Dreading my parents tomorrow," Mateo said, only half lying. "Loved yours, by the way. You're lucky."

"I'm not a very good son," Sean said, surprising Mateo. "They don't see me often."

Mateo watched the road and nodded. "I imagine most people don't see you often. Things will change when you're out of school. I'm sure they're proud of you for doing something with your life. If no one else has told you lately, I'm proud of you."

Sean touched Mateo's hand on the gearshift. Mateo didn't hesitate linking fingers with him. He glanced over. Sean stared out the window, looking lost in thought, or just lost. Sometimes, Mateo wondered if Sean was unhappy. He tried hard to change that, but he didn't think it had anything to do with him. Mateo didn't know how to start that conversation. His house came into view, pulling his thoughts in a new direction. He'd convinced Sean to stay. Could he also talk him into another kiss?

He carried Sean's bag inside. His heartbeat sounded loud inside his ears. There wasn't a single reason for Mateo to be nervous. Sean had taken countless naps, sleeping next to Mateo. In fact, nap time had become his favorite time of the day. He'd yet to fall on Sean like a love-starved sicko. Mateo doubted he'd start tonight.

Mateo tried focusing on something else as he carried Sean's bag to the bedroom. The instant he turned the light on, his gaze landed on Sean's Christmas present. Damn, he hoped Sean's pride didn't stop him from accepting. After setting the bag aside, he snagged the gift and headed back down the hall. Mateo found Sean grabbing a bottle of water from the fridge. It was such a small and insignificant thing, but Mateo couldn't stop smiling. Sean was comfortable here. Goddamn, he really wanted to keep Sean, but nothing good ever happened to Mateo. He'd given up trying for happiness years ago.

"Hey, baby. Let me see your phone."

Sean choked on his water, laughing. The sight had Mateo hard as a rock. Sean's happiness was the sexiest thing on the planet. "Why? Are you in the mood to wince and mutter to yourself?"

Mateo released a loud and weary-sounding sigh. "Please?"

With a shrug, Sean dug his phone from his pocket and passed it over.

Mateo popped the back off and removed the SIM card before setting the phone aside. He didn't look to check Sean's reaction. Instead, he pulled the new smartphone he'd bought Sean from his back pocket and inserted Sean's card. He spoke while keeping his gaze locked on his chore. "I tried to think of something you needed, because I want to make your life easier, but I would also love it if you got to enjoy something frivolous for a change. So, yes, this is the newest phone on the market, but you need it." He handed it to Sean. "Merry Christmas."

Sean didn't take it. "That's not fair. You know I can't afford to spend that much on you."

Mateo didn't think. He reacted. His feet moved. Their bodies collided. Mateo pinned Sean to the counter where he couldn't get away. "Do you know what I want most in the world?"

Sean shook his head but didn't speak. With his chin tilted up, Sean held Mateo's gaze, but he looked wary.

"You're giving it to me right now," Mateo answered. "I want your time. Your company." Mateo swallowed. Sean made him so goddamn weak and strong at the same time. "I need to know you have a reliable phone to reach me with if you need me." He stuffed the phone in Sean's front pocket, refusing to be rejected.

"Okay." Sean's agreement came out so low, Mateo wouldn't have heard if he hadn't been standing so close. "Do you want your present?"

Mateo's hunger grew. Without thought, his hands

moved to Sean's hips. His thumbs brushed the bare skin above Sean's waistband. "You mean this isn't it?"

Sean's smile melted Mateo's heart. "No. It's in my bag."

Even though he didn't want to, Mateo took a step back, freeing Sean. He didn't watch as Sean disappeared down the hall. He was afraid—if he did—he might follow. Thankfully, Sean returned before Mateo had too much time to think about it. Sean handed him a small box. It was cheerfully wrapped to perfection. He almost hated to mess up the hard work that had gone into the packaging. Nervous anticipation rolled off Sean in waves, so Mateo dug in. It was a watch. Even though it wasn't an expensive watch, it wasn't cheap either.

"I know people don't really wear watches anymore and I've never seen you wear one, this is more a sentimental piece. Flip it over."

Mateo flipped it over. The back was engraved. "Time always flies when I'm with you—Sean"

Mateo's chest tightened. He set the watch on the kitchen island and closed the distance between them. "Why are you so amazing?" Mateo asked as he gathered Sean against his chest and squeezed.

Sean wrapped his arms around Mateo and held on. His voice came out muffled against Mateo's chest. "I wish I could do more. You do so much more for me than I do for you."

That was enough of that. Sean was obviously blind because Mateo wasn't worth the space he occupied. After linking fingers with Sean, Mateo headed down the hall. He stopped by the dresser and dumped his pockets. Sean did the same. He'd been avoiding Sean's stare. His head spun. Mateo had never wanted anyone more, but he respected the hell out of Sean. Not to mention, there was something vulnerable about Sean. Mateo always feared pushing too hard or going too far. Losing Sean wasn't an option. Mateo would stay here on the edge of something huge forever if it meant he got to keep the man in some capacity.

When there was nothing left to distract him, Mateo finally met Sean's gaze. "Will you come to bed with me?"

Sean snorted out a laugh. "I already agreed to stay the night."

Mateo didn't smile or look away. "I know, but I also want to kiss you again."

The humor in Sean's expression melted away until he matched Mateo's intensity. "Okay."

"On the bed," Mateo said, motioning toward the waiting bed.

"Okay." Sean didn't look scared. Neither did he look comfortable.

"I promise my pants will stay on."

Sean nodded. "I trust you."

That made one of them.

———

THERE WAS a good chance Sean would hyperventilate. If Mateo didn't think he was pathetic, Sean didn't know why. He was certain most men were braver. Mateo was probably used to having men jump him hours after meeting him. When it came to matters of sex, Sean was a failure. Once upon a time, he'd been different. That was a lifetime ago.

Sean spent an awkward moment wondering what to do next. Mateo took control, saving him from floundering. He fingered the hem of Sean's shirt. "Can I have this?"

Sean didn't hesitate taking off his shirt. Mateo's gaze still never wavered from Sean's face, even as he pulled his own shirt up and over his head. Sean almost swallowed his tongue. Mateo spent every minute he wasn't with Sean at the gym. It showed. He was damn glad he'd taken his shirt off first or he might not have worked up the nerve to do so after seeing Mateo's body.

Mateo wiped away Sean's insecurity in an instant. "Goddamn, you're sexy." Sean might've thought Mateo was only flattering him if not for the man's eyes. The way he stared at Sean screamed he meant every word. In one quick motion, Sean found himself in Mateo's arms. The man's mouth moved against his. His teeth gnawed at Sean's bottom lip. Sean's feet left the floor when Mateo grabbed two handfuls of ass and lifted. Without thought, Sean wrapped his legs around Mateo's waist. Mateo headed for the bed.

The mattress welcomed him as Mateo climbed into bed and settled between Sean's thighs. Behind his zipper, Sean's dick begged for Mateo's touch. The man's tongue was heaven. Mateo might've promised their pants would stay on, but that didn't stop the man's hips from moving as if he was already buried root deep inside Sean. Sean gasped for air as Mateo's mouth moved from his lips to his throat. He hadn't been fucked in his clothes since high school. It was happening now. The way Mateo ground down on him massaged Sean's dick through his clothes. He already knew he'd come in his jeans. All Sean could do was try to keep it from happening too fast.

"Tell me if I scare you," Mateo said against Sean's collarbone. "I promise I'll stop."

Mateo's hands were everywhere. He had a handful of ass, holding Sean in place as he rocked against him. A thin layer of sweat coated Mateo's skin. Sean craved the flavor of the man's salt on his taste buds.

"I'm not afraid," Sean lied. He was fucking terrified, but not for any reason that would make sense to Mateo. Before Mateo, he'd had nothing to lose. Everything he owned was barely holding together. His life was pretty much empty. Then, Mateo had appeared from nowhere, and suddenly, Sean had so much to lose, he could barely breathe at the thought. Now Mateo kissed him like he felt the same, and Sean was scared shitless at how badly he wanted it.

"You're gonna come in these jeans." Sean whimpered at Mateo's claim. "Don't worry. I will too."

Sean would be the first to orgasm. He already knew it. Not only was Mateo doing amazing things to his body, it was hot as hell that Mateo wasn't the least bit embarrassed to blow in his jeans during the equivalent of a teenage make-out session.

"Fuck, Sean." Mateo's mouth opened over Sean's again. Their tongues fought. The friction of their bodies wasn't enough, yet it still threatened Sean's sanity. His entire being focused on the building ache in his cock. Mateo's mouth moved from Sean's mouth to his jaw and then to his ear. He held Sean's jaw as he tongued Sean's neck. Mateo's thumb brushed his bottom lip. Sean opened his mouth and drew the finger inside. He couldn't control himself. His tongue stroked Mateo's thumb, licking it the way he wanted to savor the man's dick.

Mateo's lips touched Sean's ear. "Goddamn," Mateo breathed. "You're so fucking hot. I want you on my dick so goddamn bad. You make me weak. All I think about is you and all the ways I want you. Damn, Sean. I can picture that tongue licking my dick." Without warning, Mateo claimed his mouth again and palmed Sean's cock through his jeans. It was as if that was what Sean had been waiting for all along. A gasp ripped from his throat, vibrating through their kiss. Ecstasy tore through him. His cock pulsed in his jeans, filling his underwear with hot cum. Mateo moaned. It was the sexiest sound Sean had ever heard in his life. Mateo pulled away and held Sean's gaze as he came. Sean couldn't close his eyes against the sight. He'd never felt more connected to anyone in his life. This was the other half of Sean's soul. Eventually, he'd have to admit it or lose Mateo forever and that wasn't an option.

5

---

*M*ateo's parents' house was three of Mateo's. It was unnerving. To keep from flipping out, Sean ran down a list of everything he'd love to have in his dream home, and still he couldn't fathom a reason for two people to need so much space. Even though Mateo swore Sean had been invited, there was a vibe in the room, making him feel unwelcome. Everything was formal. They ate at a huge dining room table on fine china. The meal was done in specific order of courses. It could've been the best food on the planet and Sean wouldn't know. Everything tasted like ash.

"What do you do for a living, John?" Renato asked from the head of the table. The man was a bit frightening. He wasn't a large man, but money and power rolled off him in waves. His dark hair never once moved from its perfect style and his gold watch cost more than everything Sean owned. Sean had never been more intimidated, and that was saying a lot.

"It's Sean," Mateo said, correcting his father.

"I'm fairly certain that's what I said," Renato said, his accent thickening as he obviously didn't appreciate being corrected. "Either way, I'm sure John knew who I meant."

Well, this was going great. "I'm in my final year at Monsieur Julliam's Culinary."

Mateo's mother, Izabella, perked up at Sean's answer. "Ooh, that's an amazing school. My friend's daughter tried getting in, but they only take the top two percent or something like that." She looked nicer than her husband, but still unapproachable. Her long black hair was in a braid over one shoulder. Her white button-down blouse was buttoned all the way to the top, reminding Sean of an old timey school teacher.

Sean nodded. "I'm very blessed."

"He means talented," Mateo said, lifting his wine and taking a sip. "He's just too modest to say as much."

Sean bit back a smile.

Renato wasn't as impressed. "You're in college? Are you even old enough to drink?"

Somehow, Sean managed a polite smile. "Yes, sir. I'm twenty-six."

"Twenty-six? Shouldn't you be out of school already?"

That clinched it. This was hell. Mateo had shown him heaven last night and then Sean had woken up in hell. He could feel the flames licking at his skin. His brain itched from being on edge for so long. If this didn't end soon, Mateo would never speak to him again, because Sean would break down.

"Oh," Izabella said, jumping in and saving Sean from having to find a way to answer. "If you're soon to be a chef, I'm assuming you know a lot about dinnerware."

He had no fucking clue why she'd think so, but whatever. Sean would gladly talk about anything—global warming, politics, religious views, or even his stance on abortion if he didn't have to explain why he was just now in college. Bullshitting his way through a dinnerware conversation sounded like fucking heaven to him.

"Sure." Even to Sean's ears, it sounded like a lie.

She clapped and came to her feet. "Renato, you should take Mateo out back and show him the latest addition to your car collection. I'll take Sean to the kitchen and show him the bowls I got at auction last week."

Car collection, as in more than two. Once again, more than two people needed. Sean wouldn't make it much longer. Sarcasm scratched at his brain. Bitterness crawled beneath his skin.

Renato smiled. It was genuine for once. "That's a great idea," Renato agreed as he came to his feet. "Come on, son. You have to see this."

Sean kept his gaze locked on a gaudy painting in the corner to keep from casting Mateo a desperate glance. This was the man's family. It was Christmas. He would not beg for Mateo to save him. Sean stood when Mateo did. Their gazes met for a second. Sean fought not to show his growing misery. Instead, he followed Izabella into the kitchen, listening to her chatter happily.

"When my mother-in-law died, she left everything to Mateo. For the most part, I didn't mind. After all, he's my son. I want him to be taken care of, but she had a china collection I adored. I'm not a chef like you," she said over her shoulder. "But I love pretty things," she added with a laugh. He tried forcing out a chuckle. "Anyhow, the set got lost or broken over the years, so I've been keeping my eyes out at auctions. Last week, I struck gold." She grabbed a stool from the kitchen island and dragged it to the sink. When she climbed on, Sean rushed over and helped steady her. She glanced down, her surprise evident. The first genuine smile he'd seen all day touched her lips. "Thank you. When we had the house built, I didn't realize these shelves would be so high." She pulled a bowl from the cabinet above the sink, passed it to Sean, and climbed down. Once she was safely on the floor, she retrieved the bowl. "Isn't it beautiful?"

It was white. There was a fine line of gold around the edge, but really, it was white. Sean smiled. "It's gorgeous." And white. Seriously. There was nothing special about it at all. Even though Sean recognized his thoughts had become ugly and unreasonable, he couldn't stop it from happening. He hated feeling out of place. Sean might work with the public, but he was an introvert at heart. He'd come here for Mateo. Sean wanted every part of the man, including getting to know his family. He felt like he was failing and it wasn't sitting well.

"You seem sweet," Izabella said suddenly while still inspecting her plain bowl. The words came out in such a kind tone, Sean almost thanked her. The hint of a "but" or something in her tone stopped him. "But..." There it was. "My son is a contender for the Super Lightweight title." She finally met his gaze. "The last thing he needs is for people to talk about his little problem." Sean blinked. He almost asked what the hell she meant, and then it dawned on him. She meant his sexuality. Sean bit back a snort. Only his good manners stopped him. Surely she couldn't be serious. Izabella kept talking, solidifying Sean's dislike. "I don't know if Mateo told you, but we're wealthy people." As if Sean couldn't figure that out by the multi-million-dollar home he currently stood in. "Just tell me what it would take to make you go away, and I can make it happen."

"Oh, wow," Mateo said from the kitchen doorway, startling Sean and making Izabella drop the bowl she'd been holding. It shattered. Sean jumped away, but he wasn't quick enough. A piece of flying glass ricocheted off the edge of the counter, hitting him in the arm, and slicing through his skin. All Sean could do was stare at the red liquid pouring from his arm. "Holy shit," Mateo said, sounding panicked as he dashed across the room. "Come here." He grabbed Sean's arm, not hesitating to put pressure on the wound as he tugged Sean toward the sink. After turning on the water, he shoved Sean's forearm beneath the flow and gently washed the wound. Sean stared at the top of Mateo's head as he inspected the cut. The room spun. He couldn't decide if it was loss of blood or the day's events making him lightheaded. Either way, he wanted to go home. "Damn, baby. This is deep. You need stitches."

Of course he did. Otherwise, this horrible day wouldn't have been complete.

"It was an accident," Izabella said, sounding on the verge of hysterics. "I was just—"

"You were just attempting to pay him off to make him go away when I walked in and startled you," Mateo said, cutting her off and using the driest tone Sean had ever heard. He never looked away from Sean's arm as he spoke. "Find me something to put pressure on this so I can take him to the hospital."

She didn't budge. "I could drive you."

"You could," Mateo agreed. "But I'd rather you didn't. Please find me a hand towel or something."

Sean couldn't stop switching his gaze between Izabella and the top of Mateo's head. She looked devastated. He sounded... dead. Finally, Izabella turned away, going in search of something to stem the blood. Without thought, Sean brushed his fingertips down Mateo's spine. His body felt harder than usual—like his every muscle was tensed to spring or snap.

"I'm sorry." Sean's words came out in a whisper. He was too scared to speak any louder. He'd never seen Mateo like this—frighteningly silent.

Mateo turned his head, meeting his gaze. If Mateo hadn't been holding his arm, Sean would've taken a step back at the fury blazing in the man's eyes. "You have nothing to apologize for."

Sean's eyes burned. His throat swelled. He'd never been scared of Mateo before. He was now. "I'd really like to go home, please?" Jesus. The fear was in his every word. Sean couldn't stop it. His voice shook and Sean hated himself for it.

While keeping pressure on his wound, Mateo straightened and shifted closer. Sean held still by force of will alone. His brain screamed for him to take a step back. "It's okay," Mateo said, his features softening. His free arm encircled Sean's waist, pulling him even closer. "I'm not upset with you. You're hurt. That pisses me off, but I'm not mad at you. This isn't your fault."

Sean tried to take a deep breath, but a short burst of shallow breathing was all he could manage. His insides shook. He had to clamp his back teeth against it while concentrating on blinking so he wouldn't look like a psycho. "I want to go home." Sean hadn't been this close to a breakdown in months. He could feel it building. The last thing he wanted was for Mateo to witness him coming apart at the seams.

Mateo's touch lightened. Concern tinted his gaze. His voice softened. "You need stitches, baby. Let me take care of you, okay? I promise to get you home as fast as possible, but you need stitches first." He pushed a stray lock of hair behind Sean's ear. The first steady breath filled Sean's lungs at the gesture. "I shouldn't have brought you here. You're so damn amazing for putting up with me." Another full breath pushed its way in. "I don't deserve you."

Sean couldn't blink. He couldn't look away from Mateo for even a second. Every word leaving his sexy lips was perfect—like he knew exactly how to reset Sean's fucked up brain.

"Here," Izabella said, shoving a dark-colored hand towel at Mateo, as if she could swat them apart. "This should work. Are you sure you won't let me drive you?" she asked as Mateo accepted the towel.

He turned his face away, but not before Sean caught a glimpse of his pain. "No, Mom. I've got this."

She twisted her fingers while staring at his back. Desperation etched her every line. "I really am sorry."

"I know," Mateo said, sounding tired. "Me too."

Sean wanted to ask why. Why would he feel as if any of this was his fault?

Izabella beat him to it. "Why are you apologizing? I'm the one who dropped that bowl."

Mateo turned the water off and wrapped the towel around Sean's arm. He kept steady pressure on the wound, yet Sean knew the man did everything possible not to hurt him. Mateo didn't answer right away. Instead, he tucked Sean's arm against his body before digging out his keys. When he finally met Izabella's gaze, his features were clear of all emotion. It was like he'd checked out from her. "I'm sorry, because I'll never be the son you wanted."

Without another word, he stepped around her, tugging Sean along with him. Sean was numb. Between his own near freak out and Mateo's barely suppressed pain, Sean's brain wasn't at full capacity. All he could do was stick to Mateo's side. One thought kept rambling through his head. For once, he wasn't the only fucked up person in the room. He didn't know whether to laugh or cry.

MATEO STARED at the blank white wall across from him and focused on his breathing. He'd once dated this yoga instructor who'd sworn any life issue could be dealt with by proper breathing alone. Personally, Mateo thought it was bullshit. At the moment, he'd try anything. The doctor stitching Sean's arm kept tossing looks Mateo's way. He wasn't sure if the man expected him to explode into a fit of rage at any moment or if he was waiting for Mateo's heart to stop. Either way, the man wasn't wrong. Mateo expected either scenario any second too.

To keep from flipping out, Mateo switched his gaze to Sean. The man was stoic and steady. He didn't even flinch with each pass of the needle. Instead, he seemed to have withdrawn inside himself, going somewhere where nothing could hurt him. The man's current calm didn't wipe away the image of his earlier panic. Mateo couldn't unsee what he'd seen in Sean's gaze while they'd waited for his mom to find a towel. Someone had hurt Sean. He didn't know if it had been the man's parents, which he couldn't picture, or a past relationship, but someone had put their hands on this sweet, amazing man. The fury was real and deep. Mateo was so goddamn enraged he couldn't pin his anger to one person. He wanted to yell, throw shit, and end someone's life. Sean didn't need him to be that person right now. So Mateo swallowed his anger and the pain from his mother's betrayal and did nothing.

"There," the doctor said as he washed away the blood. "I'll bandage this real quick and you'll be good to go. Keep it covered for twenty-four hours and dry for at least two days. After that, you can get it wet, but don't submerge the stitches in water. Come back in two weeks and we'll take them out for you for no extra charge. You don't need an appointment or anything. Just tell them out front that you got them done here and a nurse will take them out."

"Thank you."

The weight on Mateo's chest increased at Sean's sweet tone. The man shouldn't be thanking anyone for getting stitched up, for fuck's sake. He should be raging against Mateo, cursing his name for taking him into that den of hatred. Mateo tried taking another measured breath. He'd been so certain. His parents had gotten better at pretending acceptance. Mateo had hoped, if they met Sean, they'd finally understand. How could anyone resist this man sitting across from him?

"I'll take care of the bill," Mateo said the moment they were alone.

Sean's green gaze slid his way. Mateo's lips tingled with the desire to kiss him. "I have insurance."

"Yell at me." Even Mateo didn't know where the words came from, but he needed it. If Sean would scream or anything, other than this accepting silence, then maybe he could yell too. Not at Sean, of course. At life. At his parents. Maybe he'd stop feeling so goddamn trapped and helpless.

"I never would've taken the money."

Against his will, a snort escaped Mateo. "Is that what you've been sitting there thinking about?"

"It matters to me. I never would've accepted any amount of money in exchange for your friendship."

The pain sitting on Mateo's chest doubled. "Is that all we are?"

The silence dragged on as Mateo held his breath, waiting. "No." With one whispered word from Sean, everything changed.

Mateo came to his feet. The doctor came through the door, keeping Mateo in place.

"I have your discharge papers."

Mateo reached for them, giving himself an excuse to move closer. "I'll take those." He folded them up without looking at them and stuffed them in his back pocket. The doctor said something else, but Mateo couldn't focus. Sean had finally admitted they were more than friends. All the kisses and late nights weren't empty. Mateo wasn't alone. Sean shifted positions, crawling from the bed. Mateo immediately reached out to help. Their palms collided. Mateo's mouth went dry as their gazes met as well.

"I'll take you home."

Sean didn't respond right away. Instead, he held Mateo's gaze. Sometimes, he swore their souls touched. "I've changed my mind. I don't want to go home."

Mateo licked his overly parched lips. He swore he could taste Sean already. "You need to rest."

"I can do that at your place as easily as mine."

"All right." Even as Mateo's lips shaped the agreement, he knew it was a lie. He'd waited long enough. If Sean came home with him now, the man was as good as fucked—literally.

SEAN COULDN'T PINPOINT when he'd broken. Maybe it had been the hurt in Mateo's eyes when he'd realized his mother's betrayal or the devastation as he'd stared at nothing while the doctor stitched Sean up. Perhaps he'd already been lost the first time Mateo asked for his phone number. Whenever it happened, as Sean walked through the door of Mateo's million-dollar home, he knew what he wanted. It no longer mattered if Mateo was out of his reach. Sean would reach for him anyhow.

"There's blood on your shirt," Mateo said as Sean toed off his shoes inside the door.

Sean glanced down at himself. "I hadn't even noticed."

Mateo moved closer. Sean tilted his chin up and the held the man's gaze as he came to stand over him. Mateo's fingers curled around the hem of Sean's shirt. His knuckles scraped Sean's skin as he slowly slid the shirt higher. "Let me have it. I'll take care of it."

Sean's dick stirred. Goosebumps rose on his skin. He couldn't look away from Mateo's dark eyes. He dutifully lifted his arms and let Mateo have his shirt. Mateo turned away. Sean wanted to cry out at the loss of his stare.

"Go get in bed. I'll get you some juice."

Sean didn't budge. "I'm fine."

Mateo glanced over his shoulder, his expression dark. "Go get in bed."

Maybe he did need juice. His mouth was like sandpaper. Sean's feet moved without thought. Mateo's bed called his name. His cargo shorts felt like they weighed a ton. They irritated his skin. In fact, all his clothes constricted, making him want to growl in frustration. He shuffled down the hall, past the bathroom and home gym before reaching Mateo's room. He stripped as he stared at the place where Mateo slept each night. His thick dark blue comforter was balled up in the middle of the bed. Sean didn't bother smoothing it out before climbing into the massive slice of heaven. The man's ultra-expensive mattress molded to Sean's body. Sean grabbed the edge of the blanket and covered his nudity. He didn't have time to think about the repercussions before Mateo stood over him, handing him a glass of orange juice.

"It's not the same as what you make, but no store-bought juice could compete with you," Mateo said with a smirk.

Sean accepted the glass and immediately set it on the bedside table without taking a drink. He snagged the hem of Mateo's shirt and tugged. Mateo's eyes darkened. His smile disappeared. Sean had never felt more stalked than he did as Mateo set his knee on the edge of the mattress and climbed on. He pushed the comforter aside. Mateo's lips parted as his gaze moved down Sean's nude body before settling on Sean's face once more. For a moment, they simply stared at each other before Mateo reached over his head and tugged his shirt off. Sean couldn't look away. He'd seen Mateo's body before. The sight never got old. Mateo worked the button loose on his shorts before sliding his zipper down. He stopped there as if he didn't want to scare Sean away. He moved closer. Sean held still—waiting. Mateo's hard body settled between Sean's thighs. The silence between them was deafening. Neither of them tried breaking it. Instead, they simply stared at each other. Entire unspoken conversations passed between them. They'd always known they'd end up here. It had been inevitable. They'd been crawling toward this moment since the night they'd met. Sean should've stopped fighting against it a long time ago, but he was scared.

"Teo," Sean whispered, only able to push half of Mateo's name past his swollen throat.

"I've got you," Mateo swore as he lowered his head and touched his lips to Sean's.

Sean clung to Mateo's shoulders. They felt even harder than usual. The only thing soft about Mateo was his kiss. The brush of his lips was so light, Sean wanted to scream. Instead, Sean bit him. His teeth sank into Mateo's bottom lip before Sean thought about the consequences. Mateo moaned like a tortured man. Sean did it again.

"Jesus," Mateo breathed, sounding so fucking aroused Sean thought he'd come unglued. "No one has ever made me feel the way you do," Mateo said, coming at Sean from a different angle. Sean didn't know if Mateo was being honest or just mumbling whatever in the heat of the moment. He didn't care. He loved it. Their tongues entwined. Sean prayed it would never stop even as he shoved at Mateo's shorts, pushing them down the man's hips. Mateo's erection caressed his. A moan rose in Sean's throat. He'd never wanted anyone as badly. Mateo's lips moved to Sean's jaw. "I'll make you feel good."

Shit. Sean wasn't sure how much more he could take. Mateo kissed a path down Sean's chest. Sean held the man's head in a light grip. With his eyes closed, Sean savored every stroke of Mateo's tongue against his skin. He swore he felt every taste bud as they stroked across his nipple. Mateo moved lower. Some of Sean's joy fled. A hint of worry creeped in. Mateo's tongue circled his navel. Against his will, Sean's hips left the bed. He felt Mateo's muscles tense, as if he meant to shift even farther down the bed. Sean tightened his hold on Mateo's head, stopping him. Mateo's chin shot up. Their gazes met.

Sean tried swallowing past the desert that had set up shop in his throat. "You don't have to do that."

For a moment, Mateo's gaze moved over Sean's face. Sean fought back a blush. He was so turned on and he couldn't wait to have Mateo inside him. The last thing he wanted was to ruin the mood by making Mateo do something men like him didn't do. To his surprise, a Cheshire cat grin slowly spread across Mateo's face. He untangled himself from Sean's hold.

"Has no one ever sucked your dick?"

The heat Sean had been holding at bay exploded in his cheeks at Mateo's harsh wording. He shook his head. "I know men like you don't do things like that."

Mateo's lips parted before snapping closed again. His face screwed up as if working through Sean's words. "Men like me," he repeated, sounding confused. His expression cleared before turning smoldering. "Baby, this man loves sucking cock, and is about to blow your mind." While holding Sean's stare and his hands out of the way, Mateo lowered his head and licked Sean's erection from crown to root. Against his will, a pant escaped Sean. His head dropped to the pillow. Mateo shifted once more, releasing Sean's hands, spreading his thighs, and diving in.

A loud gasp flew around the room and bounced off the walls as Mateo's tongue probed at Sean's asshole. It took Sean a second to realize the sound came from him. Mateo didn't stop. He licked and prodded until Sean was practically riding his face. It was out of Sean's control. No one had ever had him so close to coming with the barest of touches. Then, Mateo swallowed his dick. All of it. He could feel Mateo's lips wrapped around his root. The man's nose buried against his body. Sean had to stop himself from flying off the bed. He scratched at the sheets, seeking purchase as Mateo set a pace Sean couldn't match. The hot pull on his cock was unlike anything he'd ever experienced. It was no wonder men always wanted this from him. Sean was nowhere near this good. Mateo was everywhere—licking Sean's dick and fingering his ass while still toying with his balls. The lower half of Sean's body was soaked in saliva and pre-cum. Sean's entire being focused on the building pressure tightening inside him. His heels dug into the mattress. Every muscle in his body tensed—expectant. Mateo kept winding him tighter until Sean couldn't breathe. Mateo sucked hard and everything exploded into pulses of color and ecstasy. Sean openly fucked Mateo's mouth, incapable of stopping. He needed every twinge of pleasure and Mateo wasn't letting up. He licked and swallowed, making tiny aftershocks pulse through Sean. Tiny mewling noises came from the back of Sean's throat. He couldn't stop them. Mateo kissed a path up Sean's body—open-mouth kisses that had Sean squirming and trying to bring Mateo's mouth to his.

When Mateo finally opened his mouth over Sean's, Sean didn't hesitate kissing him back every bit as desperately. The taste of his own cum didn't bother him. He'd never experienced such a sexy moment. Being with Mateo was porno-level good. He was what men fantasized about. Sean tried pulling the man's hips closer, needing Mateo inside him.

Mateo pulled away. His eyes looked unfocused. In fact, with his swollen lips and flushed cheeks, Mateo was the picture of aroused male. Sean's lust skyrocketed. "I need a condom, baby. Gotta keep you safe."

Yes. Condom. This was important. Sean nodded, biting back his impatience. After leaning over and digging through the bedside table, Mateo sat back on his heels and opened a gold package with his teeth. Sean had to force himself to take a deep breath as he watched Mateo roll the thin sheath down his cock. Even the muscles in Mateo's forearms moved in ways that turned Sean on. He'd never seen anyone more perfect. Every deep valley and hard muscle made Sean's mouth water. Sean was certain, before Mateo, he'd never known pure lust.

"You're so beautiful," Sean said, sounding breathless even to his ears.

Mateo smiled. His dimples made an appearance. "That's my line, baby," he said before covering Sean's body once more. Their lips met and then their tongues. Sean lost himself for a moment in the way Mateo licked and retreated before savoring. The man's fingertips skimmed Sean's thigh before he urged Sean's knee higher. His hard cock pushed against Sean's asshole, seeking entry. Against his will, Sean tensed.

"You make me wish I was a good man," Mateo whispered, shocking Sean to the point he forgot what the lower half of Mateo's body was doing. Before Sean could work up a thought to argue, Mateo pushed his way inside, stealing Sean's breath. He was larger than anyone Sean had ever been with and Sean hadn't been with anyone in a long time. He fought the urge to shove at Mateo's massive chest and scramble away. Mateo held still, giving Sean time to adjust while doing nothing more than nibbling at Sean's lips until Sean wanted to scream in frustration.

Finally, Mateo rocked forward, hitting something amazing inside Sean. He moaned around Mateo's bottom lip. Mateo held Sean's face between his hands and pulled away just enough to hold Sean's stare as he made love to him. "You shouldn't be here with me."

Sean's head was a mess. Mateo was doing earth-shattering things to his body, but the man's words didn't match his sweet actions. "I don't want to be anywhere else."

Mateo's eyes slid closed for a moment as if the pleasure was overtaking him. When his eyes opened again, Sean swore they shone brighter than before. "You deserve a good man." Mateo's voice sounded rough—like he had gravel in his throat.

"You're a good man," Sean argued, trying desperately to make Mateo believe him even as the man's cock kept pounding inside him at the perfect angle and his dick leaked on his stomach like Mateo hadn't just blown his mind. He couldn't stop himself. Sean reached between them and massaged his dick, needing to come. He was already right there on the edge.

"I'm not," Mateo argued, confusing Sean. He was too close to the edge to recall what they'd been talking about, but he completely understood the next words leaving Mateo's lips. "But I am the man who's falling in love with you."

A cry ripped from Sean's throat as another orgasm tore through him. His body clamped down on Mateo. Mateo gasped and thrust harder as his pace quickened. Throwing his head back, Mateo bared his teeth. The cords in the man's neck strained as every muscle in his body hardened. Sean was fascinated by the sight. Sean's name slipped from Mateo's lips as his shoulders slumped forward, and he melted into Sean. Without a thought for the mess squishing between them, Sean wrapped his arms around Mateo and accepted the man's weight. Breathing was overrated. He couldn't think clearly, but he wasn't insane. Mateo had definitely said he was falling in love with Sean. That meant there were two fools in this bed because Sean didn't think he was falling in love with Mateo. He'd been in love with Mateo for months.

atching Mateo sleep was one of Sean's favorite things. Sometimes, when he came over for a nap, he'd pretend to sleep until Mateo's breathing deepened and then he'd spend an hour staring at him. Yeah, it was probably a creepy thing to do, but the man was fucking gorgeous. When he was awake, Mateo was all naughty charm. Asleep, he was angelic beauty. It was fascinating.

This morning, things were different. Those gorgeous full lips had been wrapped around Sean's cock. He'd kissed that neck—bitten that shoulder. Fuck. He needed to get up and find something else to do. His dick was already hard. After slipping from the bed, Sean grabbed his bag and headed for the bathroom. He found his pj pants and brushed his teeth before heading for the kitchen. The least he could do was make Mateo breakfast. He opened the fridge. A hard body molded to his back. Mateo's scent filled his nostrils as the man's arms encircled his body. Sean's eyes fell closed as he savored every sensation.

"I woke up, and you were gone," Mateo said, kissing Sean's neck.

Sean bit back a whimper. His erection was back with a vengeance. "I thought I'd make you breakfast."

"Mhmm," Mateo hummed against Sean's throat. "I kind of hoped you'd be breakfast." Sean twisted in Mateo's arms and captured the man's lips. Mateo leaned into him as their kiss deepened, grinding his hard cock against Sean's. The doorbell rang. They both looked at the screen hanging above the fridge as it fired to life with the front door's security camera feed. Mateo's dad stood at the door—waiting.

Mateo faked a cry against Sean's shoulder. "My dick is so hard right now and my dad is at the door."

Something wicked rose inside Sean. He palmed Mateo's cock through his pajama pants. "Guess I'd better find a shirt."

"Fucking evil," Mateo groaned before stealing another deep kiss and turning away.

Sean sucked in a deep breath before trying to move. He ached with want. The brush of his cotton pants against his erection was torture, but he made it down the hall.

Sean took his time finding a shirt. He didn't want to face Mateo's dad with his dick tenting his pants. Sean heard the angry voices as he passed the staircase before reaching the living room. He slowed, not wanting to intrude.

"Just read the report," Renato snapped, sounding furious. "You are worth millions and this guy is a thief."

Sean sat on the steps. He couldn't take another step.

"I don't give a shit what you dug up on Sean. He's no thief."

Renato growled. "He stole money and a car from a guy he was dating. It's all in the police report."

"And?" Mateo sounded bored, but Sean thought he'd faint. He couldn't force a full breath into his lungs.

"And what? He's a fucking crook and you're bringing him to your mother's house for Christmas. You mark my words, son, he'll sue us over that cut. He saw an easy mark in you."

"I am easy," Mateo said, obviously attempting to give his dad a stroke.

"Goddamn it, Mateo. Everything isn't always a joke. Even if he doesn't mean you harm, he will hurt you. You have a reputation to uphold. If you ever stop fucking around and actually win a title, everyone will be talking about him and not you. You'll look like a fool."

Mateo laughed. It was so fake it hurt Sean's heart. "I thought I was a gatekeeper. That's what you've always said, so really, there's nothing to worry about."

"Pull your fucking head out of your ass," Renato roared, making Sean jump. "Stop thinking with your dick and embarrassing everyone. You're a man. Act like it. You've had your mother crying all night—the way you always do. I've never met a more selfish, ungrateful—"

"Okay, well, this has been fun," Mateo said, cutting him off. "It's always nice when you stop by for a visit. I'll walk you out."

"If it wasn't for your grandmother always coddling you."

"Yes, I know," Mateo said, sounding tired. "I wouldn't suck dick. Yada yada. Let's go."

"We should've beat you as a child," Renato said, his voice getting farther away.

"It wouldn't have helped," Mateo said with laughter lacing his voice. "I let people beat me now and I kind of like it."

Whatever retort Renato had was muffled by the door. Sean assumed Mateo had closed it in his face. For a moment, silence filled the house. Only the sound of a grandfather clock ticking in the den filled the unnatural quiet. Then, footsteps moved in his direction. Mateo came into sight. He stopped at the foot of the stairs as if he'd known Sean was there.

Mateo leaned his shoulder against the wall and stared at Sean—expressionless.

"I'm not a thief." Sean didn't know what else to say.

Mateo didn't hesitate. "I know."

"But I did do the things he said."

"It doesn't matter to me," Mateo said as if it really didn't.

It mattered to Sean. "I shouldn't have let you get blindsided like that."

Mateo's mouth lifted in one corner. The bitterness in Mateo's expression made Sean's eyes sting. "What? That? That was a typical Tuesday morning for me."

Sean fucking hated that. "Still, I should've told you everything about me before you had to hear it like that."

"So tell me now," Mateo said with a shrug.

Sean took a deep breath and picked a place to start.

"When I was a senior in high school, I went with my friend to a college party. I expected drinking and possibly drugs but never planned on meeting Dylan. He was perfect, and I was swept away. The day I turned eighteen, I moved in with him without a second thought. My parents argued against it, begging me to go to college, but I knew best." Sean swallowed around the threat of his throat swelling closed. The sick pit opening in the center of his being wasn't an unfamiliar sensation. He was exhausted from the fear and pain. "I was stupid," Sean admitted, seeing it all now. "Things changed the instant I was under his roof. I was a prisoner. He wouldn't let me see my parents and I didn't have a car or money of my own. I depended on him for everything. He wasn't the kind of abusive you see on TV. Dylan didn't pick fights to beat me down. He picked away at my brain, stripping me of everything. I was too stupid to live and too ugly for anyone else to want me. That's why I wasn't allowed to leave the house. Yet he'd bring friends over like he was proud of his project. He wanted them to see me house broken."

Sean didn't look at Mateo. Instead, he chose to stare at his hands. They were his, and they were real. If Mateo tossed him, they'd still be with him. "Eventually, I hit bottom and no longer cared if I woke up. In fact, I hoped I wouldn't. It was almost like he'd been watching and waiting for me to get to that point. That's when he brought home someone else." Sean couldn't do this. If Mateo needed the words, then Sean would rather be alone. He couldn't go back to that place. "Later that night, after Dylan fell asleep, I stole the money from his wallet and his keys. I should've just took off on foot and found the nearest phone, but I was so fucking scared and not in my right mind. The car was the fastest way out and I needed money for a place to stay because I couldn't face my parents." Sean shrugged. "The rest is pretty much what you would imagine. I was arrested. Dylan said he'd wouldn't press charges if I came home." A small smile tugged at the corners of Sean's lips. Even to him, it felt evil. "I refused." His smile fell. "Now I have a criminal record and things have been much harder than I ever dreamed." He finally met Mateo's stare. "Then I met you, and you've been like breathing clean air after being trapped in a burning building. I'm sorry."

Mateo straightened away from the wall. "Why are you apologizing?"

Sean shrugged. "For me. It was pretty much a blanket apology for this," he said, motioning toward himself. "You're amazing. I forgot for a little while that I'm a mess. No one else has ever given me that. I should go." Sean started to stand.

Mateo held a hand up, stopping him. "Do I get to talk?"

Sean nodded, feeling like an idiot. Mateo should get to have his say. After all, he'd given Sean a few months of peace. He settled back down on the steps.

Mateo smiled. Sean focused on the dimples he loved. His eyes burned. Fuck Dylan for stealing another beautiful thing from him. If there was any justice in the world, wherever he was, Dylan was dead.

THERE WAS a thick layer of pure rage coating Mateo's brain. He had money. It wouldn't take much to find this Dylan guy and destroy him. Sean was more important right now. He needed Mateo calm and accepting. Mateo knew, because that was what he'd always needed from his parents that he'd never gotten. But, Sean and he, they had each other. Whatever Sean had been through, it was the past. Mateo was his present and future. Sean had nothing but rainbows and shit coming his way because Mateo would never let ugliness touch him again. It had to start now.

"Dad showed up, and I missed my chance to tell you how fucking sexy you are when you first wake up in the morning. Of course, you're always gorgeous. But this morning, you woke up as mine and I can't stop thinking about it."

The confusion written on Sean's face had Mateo's smile turning real. Making Sean happy was fucking awesome. It was like getting lit minus the consequences.

"Wait," Sean said, as if trying to keep up. "So you're not mad at me?"

Mateo's smile was out of his control. "Not at all. Now, as for my dad, I'm always pissed off at him."

Sean still wasn't smiling. It was stabbing Mateo in

the heart. He sat down on the steps, hip to hip with Sean. "Look, everyone has a past. God help me, I hope no one is hiding around the corner with a background check on me. You'd rightfully run for your life." He took Sean's hand and held on.

"I don't know," Sean said, sounding thoughtful. "I'm pretty head over heels in love with you. It would probably take a lot to drive me away."

Sean was so goddamn brave. Mateo's heart was stuck in his throat. Beyond telling Sean, in the heat of the moment, he was falling for him, Mateo hadn't worked up the nerve to say the actual words. Sean had said them so calmly—like he had no doubts.

Rather than attacking Sean on the stairs, as he wanted, Mateo calmly stood. Since he was still holding Sean's hand, Mateo didn't leave Sean any other choice but to stand too.

"Where are we going?"

"I'm guessing you don't want to get fucked on the stairs." Sean didn't respond. Mateo glanced over. A small smile hovered on Sean's lips. Turning, Mateo walked backward, still leading Sean to the bedroom. "Spill."

Sean shook his head. "I just realized I don't care if I get fucked on the stairs. You're worried over my comfort and I..." Sean shrugged without finishing.

Mateo stopped moving. "You what?"

"I don't care about anything other than being with you."

Most people would take Sean for granted. He was that nice guy who never got the credit he deserved. Mateo would never treat him as anything less than the prince he was. He'd been unhappy for a long time— always searching for something unnamed. Mateo still didn't know what he'd been missing in his life. All he knew was—he was finally whole now. "I love you." He'd expected to feel awkward. For it to be hard. Instead, Mateo had never been calmer.

Mateo didn't have time to pat himself on the back. Sean took two steps, closing the gap between them and claiming Mateo's lips. Sean wasn't one to initiate things. This was the second time this morning he'd found his dick in Sean's hand. The man's kiss was fierce, but the way he dove his hand inside Mateo's pants had Mateo's head spinning. His back hit the wall. Goddamn. No one ever took control of him, and he'd never expected this rough treatment from Sean. He liked it, but he fucking loved being in charge.

Without giving Sean time to argue, Mateo swept the man's pants down his hips, letting gravity carry them to the floor. With Sean nude from the waist down, Mateo spun, shoving Sean against the wall before lifting his feet from the floor. He kissed Sean as deep as he could get before turning his face away.

"Hold on to me." That was all the warning Mateo gave before he licked his fingers, stretched Sean's asshole, and pushed his way inside.

Sean gasped against the intrusion. Mateo made sure it turned into a moan as he switched angles. He held Sean's hips and surged upward, taking what he needed.

"You make me so goddamn horny. Do you know how many times I've jacked off to the scent of you lingering on my pillows? You're in my fucking head, Sean."

The sounds of pure ecstasy coming from the back of Sean's throat were the only noises he made. Mateo couldn't stop talking.

"You could tell me you've killed someone and I wouldn't care. I just want to be right here, holding you and connected to you. Fuck," he cursed, trying to hang on to an ounce of sanity. "I want to watch your sexy dick bounce against your stomach like this forever. Shit, look at the way it's leaking for me. I haven't even touched your cock, and it's crying for me. Do you know what that does to my head? No one gets excited to see me. You fucking drip for me."

"Oh, god," Sean whispered, making Mateo nuts.

"And this ass. Goddamn, Sean. So tight and just sucking me inside." He stopped moving and held Sean's stare. The man's flushed cheeks and unfocused eyes drove him insane. "I could just stand here and your ass would milk me dry. That's how greedy you are for me. You can't hide it, and I fucking love it. I love you."

Sean sucked air. It sounded ragged and broken. "I love you too."

At the confession, Mateo lost all sense of reason. He fucked Sean hard—like he hated him. In truth, he wanted to crawl inside the man and never leave. His life was sick and unhealthy. Sean thought he was dirty, but he was like undriven snow compared to Mateo. His orgasm hit, nearly buckling his knees in its intensity. His cock throbbed and jumped inside Sean's ass. Mateo's gaze never moved from the gorgeous dick on Sean's stomach. Fuck, he could taste it from last night. Salt and man. He slipped from Sean's ass and dropped to his knees. Sean's cock filled his mouth without thought. He sucked and savored. His tongue swirled around Sean's crown, lapping up every drop of pre-cum. When it was gone, he licked Sean's slit, trying to get more.

"You're so goddamn delicious," Mateo swore before swallowing the man's cock. He'd get his salty reward one way or another. Patience wasn't his virtue. He played with Sean's balls and urged the man to openly fuck his face. Sean didn't get it. Mateo loved this shit. It was raw and real. Sean couldn't hide a single emotion from him while Mateo had the man's dick in his mouth.

"Tell me you love me," he demanded before tightening his throat around him again.

"I love you."

Yeah. He did. Mateo could feel it. His lips slid up and down Sean's erection, the silky skin giving under the pressure. Mateo closed his eyes, opened his throat, and let Sean pound it. Sean's short fingernails dug into the back of Mateo's neck. A roar of triumph raged through him as Sean cried out his name. A hot flood of cum filled Mateo's mouth. Mateo swallowed and sucked, trying to get it all. It still coated his tongue as he kissed Sean's stomach.

"You're so fucking amazing, baby. No one is allowed to think otherwise. Not even you."

"I love you," Sean repeated, sounding hoarse as he tried pulling Mateo to his feet. Mateo stood and captured Sean's lips before his own said something he couldn't take back—like Sean was his and he'd cut out anyone who wanted to get in between them. Even if that someone was his parents.

une...

MATEO HAD EXPECTED it to be hard to convince Sean to hang out with him at the gym now that he'd graduated and spent more time with Mateo, but he'd agreed without hesitation. In fact, he'd seemed excited at the idea of watching Mateo in action. Sean always made Mateo's head swell. When they were together, Mateo wanted to flex or throw the man over his shoulder in a show of strength before carrying Sean to bed. He didn't think Sean realized how unique that made him. Most people did their best to be unimpressed by Mateo. Sean acted as if he'd never met anyone better. The instant they cleared the door of Aden's gym, Mateo knew he wouldn't get to hang with Sean by the excitement written on Remy's face as he bounded over to them.

"Yay! It's Sean. We like Sean."

At Remy's cheer, Mateo spread his arms wide. "What about me?"

Remy waved his hand in a dismissive gesture. "Your ego is already the size of the Atlantic. No one is fluffing that. But I gave Sean that membership six months ago and we're just now seeing him."

"I think you're amazing," Sean said behind him, making Mateo smile. Damn, they should've stayed in bed. There was more than one way for him to get a workout. Sean raised his voice for Remy to hear. "I've been going to school and working full-time. Before now, I haven't had time to come in. I graduated last week, so here I am."

"That's cool," Remy said with a shrug. "Education comes first. We'll just start your membership from today on. That way, you won't lose the six months you weren't here." Remy eyed Sean. "You're not dressed to play with me."

"I really don't know what that means," Sean said, sounding bewildered and wary—like he should when Remy had the glint to his eye that he did now.

"It means I'm stealing you and dressing you like a doll so we can play. Kiss your man so we can go."

"I don't know—"

"Kiss your man," Remy repeated, cutting Sean off and stopping just short of stamping his foot.

Mateo kissed Sean, keeping him in Remy's good graces. "Go with him," Mateo said low enough for Sean's ears alone. "I promise you'll be fine."

Sean nodded. "I guess I'll be back soon," Sean said, loud enough for Remy to hear.

Mateo didn't bother looking to see if it made Remy's day. Remy had called Sean his doll. He already knew the man was over the moon about having a new project. "I love you," Mateo said, gently shoving Sean toward Remy. "Have fun."

Sean glanced over his shoulder as Remy grabbed his hand and towed him toward the door. He looked as if he was being kidnapped and Mateo was letting it happen. Mateo couldn't stop smiling. Anything Remy chose to do would be good for Sean. Everyone needed a little Remy time in their life.

Mateo didn't lose track of time the way he usually did. He sparred with Brady, one of his usual sparring partners, after running through his cardio while keeping an eye on the clock. Three hours passed before Remy and Sean returned. Sean looked shell shocked, but sexy as hell in what appeared to be a whole new outfit—shoes and all.

Remy towed him past Mateo, headed for the office. "Help me," Sean mouthed as they passed, pulling a chuckle from Mateo. Sean smiled at the sound, letting Mateo know he was joking.

Between sets, he kept one eye locked on everything Sean did. When Remy started taping Sean's knuckles, Mateo came to his feet. He made it five steps before Daniel appeared in his path.

"May I ask you something? Off the record, of course," Daniel added.

Mateo's gaze never wavered from Sean and Remy. He loved seeing them playing around. Sean didn't have that in his life. "I guess."

"Are you a weirdo stalker?"

Mateo's head whipped around and a surprised snort of laughter escaped him. "What?"

Daniel shrugged. "I'm just trying to figure you out. First, you ask me to dinner and then tell me you'd love to hook up with Isaac. You're always jumping to do things for Remy and openly flirting with death by staring at the man and flirting with him. Not to mention, Carter says you'll fuck anything that moves. Yet, I honestly believe you're completely in love with Sean. I love a good mystery and you're a conundrum."

"Huh," Mateo grunted, trying to decide if he was angry. "I'm not even sure where to start with all that." He thought it over and decided he was a little pissed off after all. "First off, I only asked you to dinner because you were new in town and I didn't want you to have to go to dinner alone. Sorry, dude, but you're not my type. Secondly, Isaac is hot. I would've been crazy not to try. And third, I do not flirt with Remy. I like Remy. A lot. As a friend. He's nice and fun to be around. I love hanging out with him. If it seems like I'm flirting, it's only because I'm flirtatious person. I don't even realize when I'm doing it half the time. As for Carter, fuck that dude. He doesn't even know me."

Daniel looked more thoughtful than contrite, which did nothing to cool Mateo's temper. "The night we went to Slip, you tried to pull Remy aside and offered to go somewhere else with him. You don't think that's a weird thing to do with someone else's husband?"

If Mateo looked as if he thought Daniel was nuts, it was because he did. "Are you insane? I've been training with Aden for years to win a title. I wouldn't fuck that up or screw over a friend like that. Remy hates Boston. I didn't want him to feel left out by choosing Slip that night, and I tried getting him away from you while asking him, because it's none of your goddamn business why he hates Boston."

Daniel scoffed. "Even Aden thought you were hitting on Remy that day."

Mateo's eyebrows drew together in his confusion. "No. He didn't." Anger got the best of him. Mateo caught Aden's eye and waved him over.

The red-haired giant who'd stolen Remy's heart and trained Mateo for the past four years moved to tower over them. "Aye?"

Mateo didn't hesitate talking it over with Aden. "Do you remember some months back when a bunch of us went to Slip, and I tried to convince Remy to go by offering to go elsewhere?"

"No."

Mateo almost laughed, because if Aden had thought he'd been flirting, he'd remember it.

Daniel jumped in. "How can you forget threatening Mateo's life over it?"

Aden looked thoughtful. He shrugged. "I threaten his life all the time, so it's hard to remember a specific time. But I can't imagine threatening him over him trying to take Remy somewhere other than Slip." Aden paused as if remembering something. "Of course, if you were standing there and Mateo was discussing it, I was probably reminding him to keep his mouth shut around you."

Daniel's expression turned thunderous. "Are you

serious? You should know by now that I wouldn't print anything negative about anyone here."

Aden nodded. "Aye, I know it, but the shit between Boston and us is personal. I don't give a shit how you feel about me, but if you care about Remy at all, you'll let that topic go." He switched his attention to Mateo. "Is that all you needed?"

Mateo nodded. "Thank you."

Aden dipped his chin. "Fine. Now get back to work. I'm not running a social parlor."

As soon as Aden walked away, Daniel surprised him by apologizing. "I'm sorry. It's crazy, but there have been times I've thought I've seen you staring at Remy in an odd way."

Mateo shrugged. "He's an odd guy, but if anything, you've probably seen me trying to figure out his secret to happiness." Mateo chose to keep the rest of his soul and walk away. He wasn't sure yet if he'd bother talking to Daniel ever again.

"You're being way too quiet."

Sean startled at Mateo's observation. "Sorry. I was lost in thought." After spending the day with Remy, Sean was overwhelmed.

Mateo reached over and linked fingers with Sean.

While keeping his gaze locked on the road, Mateo tugged and pressed his lips to the back of Sean's hand. "Did you have fun today?"

"Yes, but my pride might not ever recover," Sean admitted.

Mateo pressed his lips together as if trying not to laugh. Since the backseat of Mateo's Jeep was filled with bags and boxes from Remy dropping a small fortune on him, Sean was sure Mateo was enjoying himself entirely too much.

"Don't think about it too much. Remy loves to shop, and you gave him a partner in crime. That's priceless to him."

"I don't like people spending money on me. It makes me feel like a charity case. I'm out of my league with your crowd."

Mateo didn't respond right away. Sean appreciated more than he could say that the man didn't try trivializing his feelings. "You know," Mateo said, making Sean wonder if he was about ruin Sean's appreciation. "I wish you could see how much you give other people. You think people see you as a project, but that's not true. People want to do nice things for you because you're nice, and too few people really are."

Sean stared at Mateo's profile while seriously considering calling bullshit. "I meet more nice people than mean people every day and I don't have the slightest interest in showering them with gifts."

Mateo shook his head, looking serious. "You meet a lot of people who are nice because they're wearing their in-public face. A vast majority of people are selfish assholes. You're not. When someone talks to you, you genuinely care about what they're saying. You make people want to give you as much as you're giving them with just your kindness."

"That's a nice thing to say," Sean said, because he had nothing else. He didn't think anything Mateo said was true, but he appreciated his effort.

"You don't sound like you believe me."

Sean shrugged, even though Mateo wasn't looking at him. "I know you're trying to make me feel better."

Mateo growled. Sean flattened his hand against his stomach at the sound. He should be exhausted after his first boxing lesson, but the more he had of Mateo, the more he wanted. "I could sneak some money into Aden's office if that would make you happy."

"It would."

A surprised-sounding bark of laughter came from Mateo. "It would hurt Remy's feelings."

Sean huffed. "Fine, then. I'll keep the damn gifts and my mouth shut."

Mateo cut his eyes at Sean. "I'd very much like for you not to keep your mouth shut. I love your mouth."

Sean's mind shifted gears. A rush of heat hit Sean. "If this console wasn't between us, I'd show you what my mouth can do."

Mateo's head whipped around. No one was more shocked than Sean. Mateo was the dirty talker, and Sean fucking loved it, but Sean was too shy for that. The words had popped from him before he'd known it would happen. "We're almost home."

"Watch the road," Sean warned rather than responding.

Mateo did as told, but he didn't let the topic go. "I need a shower. You should take one with me."

"You do have a large shower," Sean said, purposely avoiding answering. A dimple appeared in Mateo's cheek. Sean couldn't look away. He loved this man. All the time he'd spent avoiding entanglements and nursing his broken spirit hadn't saved him from Mateo. He'd been certain he could and would live the rest of his life in peaceful solitude. Now he couldn't imagine going back to being alone. More than that, he was barely put together. If he lost Mateo, he didn't think he could scrape the pieces of his mind together again.

Mateo pulled his keys from the ignition, making Sean realize they were home. They carried his bags of new clothes inside and left them in the living room. After dropping the final one, Mateo took his hand and headed down the hall. Sean stared at Mateo's back. His heart overwhelmed his brain. He picked up the pace and overcame Mateo as they reached the bedroom. Sean wrapped his arms around the man's waist. Mateo stopped. Sean pressed his cheek to Mateo's back and held on. The man's scent, heat, and the sound of his heartbeat were the reasons Sean got up in the morning. He spent a moment memorizing each.

"I love you," Sean whispered, needing Mateo to feel it.

Mateo relaxed into Sean's hold. "I love you too. Are you okay?"

Sean nodded, squishing his cheek against Mateo's back. "I'm stealing a moment and thanking God I found you."

Mateo turned in his arms. His fingers traced Sean's jaw. Sean fought the urge to close his eyes and savor every sensation. With the barest touch, Mateo tilted Sean's chin up and kissed him. It was a sweet gesture of lips brushing lips. Mateo pulled away before deepening their kiss. His expression had Sean scared to blink. "I'm selfish. Give me all your moments. I want them." As he made the demand, Mateo slid Sean's shirt up. Sean raised his arms, letting Mateo have his way. Once he was bare from the waist up, Mateo stared down at him expressionlessly. It was as if the man's mind had gone elsewhere. He turned away. Sean blinked at his back. Mateo moved to the dresser, opened the top door drawer, and dug around. As far as Sean could see, he came back empty handed, doubling Sean's confusion. Mateo hovered over Sean once more.

"What—"

Mateo dropped to his knees. The question died on Sean's lips. He stared down the line of his body at Mateo's upturned face. The man's eyes looked softer than usual—vulnerable. Sean's heart sped. He was near to bursting with love for this amazing man.

"I love you."

Sean's heart turned over in his chest. It was as if Mateo read his mind. Sean didn't hesitate giving the words back. "I love you too."

"You're all I ever think about," Mateo added, making Sean's eyes sting. "In less than two months, I'm fighting for one of boxing's biggest titles. It's been my dream to win that spot for as far back as I can remember, and still, all I think about is you. I'm not even nervous, because you're in my head—soothing me."

Sean wanted to cry, and he also wanted to sit on the floor so Mateo would stop telling him all this from his knees. But the fact that Mateo would stare up at him, as if humbling himself for Sean while describing his love; it was the most moving moment of Sean's life.

"You're the one for me," Mateo said, stealing a tear from Sean. He tried swiping it away, but another replaced it. Mateo's gaze never wavered as he added, "I know you are. That's why I'm on my knees, begging you to marry me."

Shock rendered Sean mute. He was slow to notice Mateo held a ring. This hadn't been spontaneous. Mateo had thought this through. Bought a ring. He couldn't take the difference in their stances any longer. Sean gave in and sat on the floor. "You shouldn't have to beg for anything from anyone. Not ever. I'd already decided you'd have to throw rocks at me if you want me leave, so this is better."

Mateo stared at him as if scared to hope. "Was that a yes?"

Sean nodded. "That was a yes."

It was a solemn moment as Mateo took his hand and slid on the ring. Sean stared down at it. It was black with diamonds circling the center. Everything about the moment was perfect.

"Who should we tell first?" Mateo asked, sounding happy. For Sean, his question was a true testament to how shitty the man's parents were. Any normal person would think to call them first. Right now, Sean just wanted to bask in the moment with Mateo. The rest of the world would intrude soon enough.

He met Mateo's gaze. "We can tell anyone you want later. First, I want you to make love to me."

Mateo's smile transformed, making him appear wicked. "Anything you want is yours."

"I was promised a shower." Sean couldn't stop. He wasn't a bold person. Mateo did something to him. Set him free.

Mateo pointed at the floor. "Stay here. I'll be right back." He hopped to his feet and headed for the bathroom. Sean stared at his back, fighting the urge to chase him down and pounce. Mateo returned a moment later, shirtless. He helped Sean to his feet. "Your shower is waiting."

Fingers linked, they walked to the bathroom together. Sean's erection fought to crawl out of his underwear. He loved Mateo's body, and the man was stripping it bare. Sean didn't move. Steam filled the large bathroom and Mateo was right there, tempting him to do everything. Still, he waited. Mateo closed the distance between them and pushed Sean's shorts down his hips. Sean realized that was what he'd been waiting for. He loved the care Mateo took with him. The way Mateo babied him was so damn addictive. His whole life he'd been starved of this. Even though Sean was a capable and independent person who could and would take care of himself, he needed Mateo's brand of affection. This man was always what he needed.

"Tell me what you want most in life and I'll find a way to give it to you."

At Sean's demand, Mateo slowly lifted his gaze from what his hands were doing to Sean's face. His expression was serious as if Sean's tone warned him how much this conversation meant. "You're what I want most. This," Mateo said, motioning between them. "Us. The happy home I never had before you gave it to me."

In that moment, Sean silently made a vow. Mateo would have everything he wanted. Sean would fight for him, even on the days Mateo didn't want to fight for himself. He would be brave again because Mateo needed someone to stand up for him.

———

SEAN WAS ALMOST ALWAYS SERIOUS. Mateo had never seen him be more so than he was right now. The man looked ready to go into battle. Mateo needed him ready to get fucked. He'd planned for weeks to take Sean on the perfect date and pull off the perfect proposal. Then Sean had wrapped his arms around him and held on. Mateo had known—that was their moment. He couldn't wait another day to make Sean his in the most permanent way. Mateo couldn't let him get away.

While still holding Sean's stare, Mateo slid his fingers down the man's cock with the lightest touch.

"You should get in the shower." When Mateo had built his house, he'd chosen the most badass shower on the market. It was part shower, part jetted Jacuzzi. The thing had built in seats, handheld massagers, and over ten hydro-massaging jets. The thing even had foot massagers and a rainfall ceiling. It was the perfect sexual torture device. As Sean climbed in, Mateo's hunger grew. He loved spoiling Sean in every way. If he could give the man three orgasms to his one, it was a good day. He planned for a great day.

There was no place to escape the water. It ran between their bodies as Mateo overcame Sean inside the shower. Their mouths collided. Mateo went deep, needing all of Sean as he walked him backward toward one of the seats. At the edge, Mateo pushed, forcing Sean to sit even as he continued licking the man's tongue. With Sean where he wanted him, Mateo reached between the man's legs and adjusted the jet, ensuring the water would stroke the man's dick with the perfect pressure. Sean gasped against his lips. A chuckle that sounded evil, even to his ears, escaped Mateo.

"Don't move and don't come yet," he ordered as he took a step back. He took a moment to eye his handiwork. Sean white-knuckled the edge of the seat and his eyes looked unfocused. He looked horny as hell and already on edge. Damn, Mateo loved a good bout of torture. He grabbed the shampoo and squirted some in his hand before returning to Sean's side. Sean's hair was shaved in the back but long on top. Mateo ran the shampoo through Sean's hair, gently washing it. Since Mateo kept his shaved short, it barely took a pass with the shampoo to clean his. Sean's heated gaze never wavered from Mateo's face. Mateo wondered over the man's thoughts. Did he picture himself doing naughty things to Mateo? Mateo hoped so because they had all the time in the world.

With their hair clean, Mateo went for the body wash next. As he lathered Sean's skin, the man moaned like he was dying. "Are you close?" Mateo asked, trying to keep the humor from his voice. "The jets in this thing are amazing. Do you know, the person working in the showroom where I ordered it was actually telling people it was the perfect self-love shower. At the time, I kind of rolled my eyes and thought it would be perfect for sore muscles, because I have more of that in my life. But now, I'm so damn glad I listened, because you look ready to explode. Watching this jet massaging that sexy dick. Jesus, this thing was worth every penny. We need to figure out how you can sit on my cock and have that thing jacking you off."

In an unexpected move, Sean shot forward and licked Mateo's hard cock. Mateo froze and stared down at Sean taking control. The nerve endings in his crown came alive as Sean teased them with his tongue. Sean's touch was so light, it was maddening. In a few short seconds, Sean already had Mateo fighting the urge to pull his hair, holding the man in place to fuck his throat.

"Holy shit," Mateo hissed, locking his hips to keep from attacking Sean. "Come for me," he begged, because he needed Sean to break. A cry vibrated around his dick and Mateo lost it. Taking his cock in hand, he jacked off even as Sean kept his lips locked around his crown. He wanted both. His mind was a sex crazed mess. This wasn't enough. There was no place better than inside Sean. He pulled Sean to his feet, spun him around, and bent him over in one quick move. Mateo spread Sean's ass cheeks and shoved his way inside. Their mixed cries sounded loud inside the enclosed shower. Bending at the knees, Mateo thrust hard and deep, nearly lifting Sean off his feet each time. He wanted to more than fuck him. Mateo wanted to become part of Sean. The man was so damn hot and tight. Mateo could fuck him all day. The need to come overrode that desire. The building pressure in his dick exploded into an orgasm powerful enough to buckle his knees, nearly taking him down.

"Sean, oh my god," Mateo gasped. "You're fucking perfect." Even to his own ears, Mateo sounded blown away. He thrust once more, needing the aftershocks.

They weren't done. The itch of addiction owned him. He needed to ruin Sean for all others—to keep him this side of madness. He lightly slapped Sean's ass. "Get moving, baby. I want you back on that seat with the water massaging that dick. You have a long night ahead of you, and several orgasms to go."

A tired-sounding laugh escaped Sean as he did as ordered. "You're an evil man."

Mateo shrugged as he moved in for a kiss. "Maybe, but I'm the good kind of evil and I'm yours." Forever, Mateo silently added, because it was true, but he didn't want to scare Sean with his intensity. He'd never wanted to take over someone's life and completely own them the way he did with Sean. They were the relationship he didn't know he needed, and now he didn't think he could live without.

8

*S*ince Sean's graduation, he still spent way more time away from Mateo than he liked. Boston got his investment out of Sean. Still, Sean woke up beside Mateo, sometimes going to the gym with him, and he went to bed beside him each night. At some unnamed point, Sean ended up with more clothes at Mateo's than at his apartment. When his lease had come up for renewal, Mateo had suggested it would make more sense financially if Sean let the apartment go. Even though Sean wasn't sure exactly how it happened, he wasn't a fool. Sean knew Mateo had maneuvered him into living together. In truth, though, it did make financial sense. Sean hadn't slept a night in his apartment since Mateo kissed him under the mistletoe. Not to mention, they were getting married. There was no reason to pretend he wouldn't eventually end up under Mateo's roof anyhow.

Tonight had been one of those nights. Slip had been slammed with people and being in the kitchen meant Sean worked twice as hard as he had on the floor. The only difference was, he no longer had to be nice to people. He still was. It wasn't in his nature to be mean. Either way, his whole body ached, and all Sean wanted was to crawl in bed next to Mateo. Unfortunately, he heard Renato's hateful voice the instant he came through the door.

Renato was another thing Mateo had been right about. His father did show up every Tuesday morning to yell at Mateo. Mateo always turned up the music in the kitchen while Sean made breakfast and begged Sean not listen to the hate. He always came back smiling after escorting Renato out, but his eyes told a different story.

Today wasn't Tuesday, and it wasn't morning. Plus, Sean hadn't seen any strange cars in the driveway. One cautious peek into the living room set him somewhat at ease. Renato wasn't there. Mateo had him on speaker phone. Sean tried ducking out of sight, leaving Mateo in private for his call. Mateo glanced up, spotting him before he could get away. He waved Sean into the room. Sean tried not to listen to Renato's tirade as he accepted Mateo's kiss. Mateo pulled him into his lap, leaving Sean no choice but to stay.

"As I told you last time, son, we'll not be wasting our hard-earned money on a Vegas trip to see you lose. Not even for a title match."

Sean tried not to let the hatred grow in his heart, but it was hard.

"I offered to pay your way," Mateo said, sounding tired, as if this was the third time he'd said the words.

"It's also the cost of our wasted time," Renato said, sounding the same as Mateo.

"I'm not asking you to be proud of me, or support me in any other way, but I'd like to have you there in my corner."

"No." Sean flinched at the cold answer. His eyes stung. Mateo's rejection felt like his own. "I have to go." Without waiting for Mateo's response, the phone fell silent.

Sean held still, wondering if Mateo would fly into a rage, and unsure if he wanted him to or not. Sometimes he thought if Mateo would break some shit, he'd feel a lot better. The silence in the room went on for so long, Sean wondered if he'd cry. He'd never hurt so much for another person and Mateo just held tight to his pain—never letting anyone see it.

Mateo's grip was almost painful. He cleared his throat. "It turns out I have two extra tickets to the title match, if you know anyone who'd like to go. I'd hate to waste them."

"What about Remy and Aden?" Sean offered, hoping he could find a way to lift Mateo's spirits.

"Aden's my trainer. He has his own set of tickets."

Sean nodded. That made sense. "I'd say Isaac and Daniel, but I noticed you haven't been talking to Daniel." Sean hoped his observation would give Mateo a chance to open up. It didn't happen.

"Daniel has press passes."

"Oh. I didn't think of that," Sean said, feeling defeated. "Don't worry over it. I'll make sure those seats aren't empty. If nothing else, I'll cheer so loud, they'll threaten to boot me."

"I love you."

Sean fucking hated how sad Mateo sounded saying those words. "I love you too."

"Did you have a good night at work?" Mateo asked, obviously hoping to change the subject.

Sean let it happen. "It was busy. I'm dead."

Mateo nodded. His expressionless face was stabbing Sean repeatedly in the heart. "Me too. All the extra training is killing me. I left you something to eat in the microwave. Will you be upset if I go on to bed?"

The pressure sitting on Sean's chest increased. He shook his head. "Go on. I need a shower and you know

I can't sleep right away. Get some rest and I'll join you in a few."

A muscle jumped in Mateo's jaw. Sean wondered if he'd snap. Instead, Mateo nodded. "I'll see you in a little while." Mateo kissed him. For a second, Sean got to pretend nothing was wrong, and then it was over. Mateo's defeated expression returned. Sean slipped from the man's lap before he lost his shit. The moment Mateo was gone, Sean released his pent-up breath. It sounded like a gunshot in the otherwise silent room. He'd never felt more useless. Sean cast a desperate look around the room, searching for any answer. His gaze landed on two tickets on the coffee table. They were the ones Mateo had been trying to give to his parents. Sean scooped them up and headed for the door before his courage fled. Maybe he couldn't fix everything, but he could try.

By the time Sean reached Mateo's parents' house, he could feel his blood pressure rising. His heart raced and blood pounded in his ears. He was certain no matter what else happened, he'd definitely faint before it was over. Sean wasn't a fighter like Mateo, but he would go to battle for his man. When it came to his parents, Mateo always kept his cool. Sean wondered if it wasn't time someone flipped the fuck out.

Most the lights were out inside the house. Sean's heart fell. He didn't think he'd have the same righteous anger driving him if he waited until tomorrow. Sean almost turned around. The lit-up garage caught his gaze and stopped him. Sean made his way toward it. He spotted Renato a half second before the man spotted him. Mateo's father faked a smile. Sean didn't bother.

"Is Mateo with you?"

Sean shook his head. "I came alone."

The fake smile remained. "That's fine too. What brings you by?"

Sean held up the tickets. "I brought these for you. This fight is important to Mateo. I'm sure you wouldn't want to miss it."

Renato's smile finally melted away. His true colors peeked through. "I've already told Mateo we wouldn't make it."

He wasn't there to play games. Sean nodded. "I'm aware."

"Then why are you here?" Renato asked, dropping the cordial tone.

"Because your son wants you to come to Vegas," Sean said, refusing to back down. "Look," Sean said, trying his damnedest not to yell. "I know you love your son. You wouldn't show up every Tuesday without fail to scream at him if you didn't. You would've walked away already. What will it hurt to go to Vegas? Do this one thing for him."

Renato shook his head. "As I've already told Mateo, we can't support his life choices."

Mateo was the most amazing person on the planet. Out of everyone in the world, the man standing in front of him should know it. "Which life choice can't you support? His boxing or me?"

Renato shrugged. "Take your pick. He's breaking his mother's heart by being with you."

Ouch. That hurt, but Sean was a master of pretending he wasn't broken. "Is that because you think I'm a thief or because I'm a man?"

"Take your pick," Renato repeated.

Sean nodded, fighting the urge to say things he couldn't take back. "I don't know what it's like to have kids, so I don't know what's right. But I do have amazing parents, and I guess they've spoiled me, because no matter what their personal opinion is on a matter, they've always put me first. If they hate the way I turned out, they've never said as much. That's all Mateo wants from you, but I see you're incapable of giving it." Sean held the tickets out. "Nonetheless, I'll leave these tickets here and hope you can find a way to put your child first."

Renato didn't take them. He shook his head. Even though he didn't look angry, as Sean expected, neither did he bend. "Keep them and give them to someone who'll go. I know you don't understand, but we won't support this."

Sean nodded. His heart broke. He'd done all he could do. "I'm sorry for you then, because you're losing an amazing man. If he wins this fight, and you have a change of heart later, he'll always wonder if you only love him for that. That's sad for too many reasons to name." Sean walked away before he cried. He hated looking weak when in truth he was furious. Sean didn't think he'd ever been more enraged in his life, and he'd been given lots of shit to rage about.

As he drove away, Sean didn't head toward home. He couldn't climb into bed with Mateo, knowing he'd failed him. An idea hit and stayed. If he couldn't give Mateo the parents he wanted, he'd give Mateo the parents he deserved. He pulled over and called his mom. She answered on the first ring, sounding panicked and making him feel like shit.

"Sean, what's wrong?"

"No, Momma. I'm okay. Sorry to be calling so late. I had to work late."

She blew out a relieved-sounding sigh. "Don't apologize for calling when you can. I'm just not used to you calling past ten. Did you have a good night at work? How's Mateo?"

He smiled. The wretchedness of Mateo's parents made him realize how lucky he was to have such amazing parents. "It was okay, and Mateo is good. Actually, he's the reason I'm calling. I know this is short notice, but Mateo is fighting for the Super Lightweight title this weekend in Vegas."

"That's amazing," she cheered, interrupting. "Please let him know how proud we are. Win or lose, that's an awesome accomplishment. He's worked so hard."

Sean's throat burned. He wished he was recording this. Mateo needed to hear it from someone other than him. Sean cleared his throat. "Actually, we have two extra tickets and would love to pay the way for you and Dad to come watch the match. Mateo needs someone cheering for him."

His mom didn't answer right away. Sean's heart fell. He'd gotten his stubborn pride honestly, and now he knew how Mateo felt every time the man tried doing anything for him. This was important. It would take all of Sean's savings to get his parents to Vegas, but those seats wouldn't be empty if it was the last thing he did.

"I don't know, Sean. That's a lot of money."

"Please, Mom." He was above begging or guilt. "Mateo's parents are refusing to go."

"Why would they do such a thing? That's their son, and I know they have the money." She said the words with such disdain, Sean knew he had her, but still. His voice broke as he made the confession.

"It's my fault. They're not coming, because he loves me."

MATEO HADN'T SLEPT at all. He was hurt and angry to the point he no longer knew which emotion would win. For years, Mateo thought one day he'd no longer care. It hadn't happened yet. All he had was Sean. The man loved him enough for three people. Mateo swore it would be enough. Sean deserved better than the way he'd acted tonight, storming off to bed and leaving him alone as if Sean hadn't just walked in the door and Mateo hadn't missed him all day.

Aggravation boiled inside him. Mateo threw back the covers, determined to hunt Sean down. It had been three hours since he'd gone to bed. There was no reason for Sean not having joined him unless he was angry with Mateo for Mateo's abrupt treatment. Fuck that. He might be a failure as a son, but he wouldn't fail Sean. Goddamn. Someone needed to be on his side. Otherwise, what was the point?

Mateo stormed the living room, determined to make things right. His feet froze to the floor. Three sets of eyes swung in his direction. "Um," he stuttered, cupping his hands in front of his dick. He was wearing underwear, but still. It wasn't every day a man showed off his bulge to his future in-laws.

Sean smiled, not bothering to hide his humor over Mateo's current circumstances. "Clothes, baby."

"We're not looking," Robin promised. Sticking true to her word, Scott and she kept their eyes glued to whatever they had spread out on the coffee table.

Walking backward until out of sight, Mateo quickly retraced his steps and found a pair of workout shorts before returning to the living room. Curiosity ate him alive. Neither of Sean's parents could see well enough to drive at night and Sean had claimed he was exhausted. He couldn't think of a single reason they'd be up at one o'clock in the morning, working on something in Mateo's living room.

"Did I miss something?" Mateo asked the moment he returned. He regretted his question as quickly. The last thing he wanted was to make Sean's parents feel unwelcome. To his relief, all three faces were smiling.

Robin was the first to speak up. "We didn't mean to bother you. Scott and I got to talking, and we realized we don't have much time to get things done before your fight, so we came on over."

At her claim, Mateo's gaze moved to what they were doing. Poster boards lined the table. One for each person. They'd drawn huge bubble letters, spelling out different cheers for Mateo.

"They're for your match," Robin explained.

Mateo blinked. His vision blurred and his chest ached. He cleared his throat past the rapid swelling. "You're making me signs?"

Her smile never wavered, but Scott answered. "Of course. You can't have a real cheer section without signs. Back when Sean played tennis, I can't tell you how many matches we got thrown out of," Scott said with a laugh.

Sean groaned. "It was horrifying."

Robin tsked. "I was in labor with you for thirty-seven hours. If I want to show my ass at a sporting event, I will, because I earned it."

Sean shook his head. "I'm not complaining. Just pointing out the obvious. It was horrifying."

"I know you're not complaining. You're a good son." She looked up at Mateo still hovering over them. "Sean's never been one to complain. He's a stoic survivor."

That he was. He was also amazing. Mateo didn't know what to say. No one had ever made a big deal of his matches. Mateo cleared his throat again. He couldn't understand why his voice didn't want to work properly. "It's pretty hard to get tossed from a boxing match."

Scott and Robin nodded. Both kept their gazes locked on their task, but Scott was the one to respond. "Don't worry. We'll give it the ol' college try."

Mateo shook his head, still unsure of how to react. "Would you like something to drink?"

Robin flashed him a smile. "We've got it covered." She held up a bottle of wine he hadn't noticed earlier. "We hit the liquor store before they closed. Sean has already gotten us set up for the night in one of the upstairs bedrooms. You two should go on to bed while we finish up. Sean has to work tomorrow and I know you have to be working your ass off this close to your match. We can entertain ourselves."

Sean stood before Mateo could respond. "Okay. If you want, you can go to bed too. We have time to do this in the morning before I go to work."

"We'll see how we feel after this bottle," Robin said with laughter lacing her words. Sean bent and kissed her cheek before circling the table to hug his dad. They were acting as if this was a normal night—like their project was nothing special when it meant the world to Mateo.

Sean took his hand. "Goodnight, guys," he called as he tugged Mateo toward the door.

"Goodnight," Robin called after them. "Love you boys."

"Yep, love you boys," Scott said, following his wife's words.

"We love you too," Sean said for them both.

Mateo stared at Sean's back as he led him back to bed. Sometimes there were no words strong enough for how much he loved this man. This was one of those moments. They'd been engaged almost two months and hadn't yet talked about when they'd get married. Now, Mateo knew. "Since your parents are going to Vegas with us, I'd like to get married before the fight on Saturday."

Sean turned and walked backward to the bed while holding Mateo's hands. "I love that plan."

Now that Sean had agreed, Mateo wondered if he was screwing Sean out of the big wedding he deserved. Sean should be publicly celebrated. "Unless you want a big wedding," Mateo said, rushing to fix things.

Sean climbed in bed, urging Mateo to join him. "No. As long as you're there and my parents are there, that's all I need. I don't like being the center of attention. Oh, we should do something crazy—like that roller coaster wedding place or the mobster wedding."

Mateo couldn't stop smiling. Minutes earlier, Mateo's mood couldn't have been darker. That was what loving Sean was like. He made everything better.

"I could see myself getting married on a roller coaster. In fact," Mateo said, climbing on top of Sean and settling between the man's thighs. "If I'd known that was a thing, I would've insisted on it from the beginning." Sean looked completely at peace and happy beneath him. "Am I making you feel rushed?"

Sean's expression never changed. "Nope. Not at all. I would've married you the night you asked if you'd been willing."

They felt like partners. That was the biggest addiction for Mateo. No one made him feel anything but alone before Sean. "I'm willing. Let's go right now."

A sexy-sounding chuckle escaped Sean. "There's a waiting period here. By the time we made it through that, we'd already be in Vegas."

"What are your parents doing tomorrow? Let's leave tomorrow, get married, and enjoy a few days before my fight."

Sean eyed Mateo, making Mateo feel as if he saw too much. "What about your last-minute training?"

"I'm ready for my match. This is what I need the most."

Sean nodded. "In that case, I'm certain my parents would be fine with leaving tomorrow, and Boston is a sucker for love, so I'm sure we could pull it off. Is there a reason for this sudden rush to the altar?"

Mateo's insides shook when he looked too closely at things. "I can't let you get away. You're too amazing for me." He'd never been more scared of losing anyone or anything in his life. If his parents couldn't love him, how could someone like Sean? He had to marry the man before Sean figured out Mateo was worthless and ran for the hills.

Sean's fingertips skimmed the back of Mateo's neck, soothing him. "You can't lose me. I'm unloseable. You're stuck. Sorry. You will be telling our grandkids one day about us getting married on a roller coaster."

"Grandkids?"

Sean shrugged. "Or not. Whatever. As long as I have you, I'm good. The rest we can figure out as we go. No matter what, we're in this together, Teo. I want to be your husband. More than that, I'm proud of being with you. You're the best part of me."

Mateo caressed Sean's ass. "So? Tomorrow, then?"

The sound of Sean's breath catching as Mateo dragged his shorts down one hip had Mateo hard enough to bend steel. "Yes. Tomorrow," Sean said, sounding breathless.

"What can I do for you tonight?"

The way Sean bit his lip had Mateo ready for anything. Sean was always sexy. When he was shy, he was irresistible. "I'd love for you to make love to me," Sean said, sounding heartbreakingly sweet. Just like everything about Sean.

Mateo shifted positions and slowly undressed him. He intended to give Sean his wish to the letter. Their nude bodies molded perfectly as their lips clung.

Mateo's heart was always full when he held Sean. He touched every place he could reach as he tasted Sean's tongue. Sean's teeth tugged at Mateo's bottom lip, making his dick twitch. Their cocks rubbing together between them created the most delicious friction. Mateo couldn't stop rocking himself against Sean.

"You were meant for me," Mateo whispered against Sean's lips between kisses. "Feel how perfect we are together," he demanded as he pivoted his hips. "Do you remember that time I made you come in your jeans? I consider that our first time together," he admitted. "It doesn't matter I wasn't inside you. We were connected. Just like we are right now." Mateo had to take a breath. Sean felt too good against him. Like every time they were together, Mateo's tongue wouldn't stop moving. "You have no idea how hot it makes me, knowing you'll have my last name by this time tomorrow." Mateo kissed Sean deep because he needed the connection. He never got enough of Sean. When it came to the man beneath him, there was a hint of insanity in the back of Mateo's mind, urging him to take over every aspect of Sean's life. That madness scratched at his skin now, wanting to be set free. Reaching between them, Mateo palmed both their cocks and stroked.

"Tell me what you need right now. Is the sensation of my palm and my dick against your erection enough?

Or do you need my cock stretching your asshole and riding you deep?"

Sean's hips lifted, meeting Mateo's stroke. "Don't stop."

Sweat had their bodies slipping against each other. Mateo tightened his hold, pulling a gasp from Sean. "I'm not stopping. If I don't feel your hot cum coating my stomach soon, I think my lungs will fail. You're my oxygen. I can live without everything except you."

"Teo, you're killing me," Sean gasped, sounding crazed. The way he writhed beneath Mateo said a lot about how close he was to the edge. Mateo needed Sean to get there. Otherwise, he'd be coming first, and that wasn't happening on his watch.

"Come on, baby. Give me a show. Make my mouth jealous. You know how I love to feel your dick jumping against my tongue. Make my mouth water and see what it's missing. Come for me."

Sean moved against Mateo's palm, straining to get there. Mateo couldn't stop staring at him, enjoying every nuance as the pressure built. He increased the pace. His brain couldn't take the teasing. He needed release. Mateo bit his lip, straining toward the ecstasy he only experienced with Sean. There was no other person alive, toy, or solo act that compared to having Sean in the same room. Even if they sat feet apart and masturbated together, it was powerful. His orgasm hit.

Mateo gasped as the burst of relief rolled down his spine. His cock jerked in his hand. His focus narrowed to his own pleasure. It wasn't until the last spasm passed that he realized Sean was right there with him. He didn't know if they'd come at the exact same time, but he wasn't surprised. He hadn't been talking shit in the heat of the moment. They were perfect together— like he could see a greater plan in the works. No matter what life threw his way, Sean would be there.

*M*ateo's phone rang the moment he gave Sean his first kiss as his husband. The first time, he ignored it. There was nothing more important than his crazy wedding, which turned out better than Mateo ever imagined. The fact that he was marrying Sean was the first thing, making it the best ever. Sean's parents came in second. The pair acted as if it was a dream wedding they'd planned themselves. Robin cried. Scott gave him the "if you hurt my son, I'll kill you" speech. Mateo hadn't stopped smiling the entire time. Never in his wildest dreams would he have pictured his wedding the way it went down. He wouldn't have had it any other way, especially since he'd never seen Sean happier. Mateo had also never expected to find love, but here he was.

The chapel was efficient. They'd even managed the perfect cake. The two grooms on top looked so much like them, they kept freaking Sean out until Robin hid it in her purse. His phone rang for the fourth time while Mateo tried cleaning squashed cake from his face while Sean tried kissing it away.

It wasn't until they were sequestered in their suite and Mateo was waiting for Sean to finish his shower that he remembered to check his phone. He'd missed six calls from his dad and two from his mom. Mateo did what he should've done a long time ago. He blocked them without listening to their messages. They'd given him life and a roof for eighteen years. He'd tried to be grateful and clung to that connection. Mateo had craved their love and acceptance. He'd never get those things from the two people he needed it from the most. It was time to move on. He'd found new connections. Blood might be thicker than water, but sometimes that only meant it would drown a person faster. They couldn't love him for him or forgive him for things he couldn't change. He couldn't be anyone else.

The bathroom door opened. Sean stepped out, wearing only boxer briefs with beads of water clinging to his skin. Mateo took a deep breath, hoping to calm his body's immediate reaction. Marrying Sean had an unexpected effect on Mateo.

Possessiveness ruled him. Sean was his. Permanently. He wanted to make his mark and scream it at the top of his lungs.

Sean caught him staring and flashed a shy smile. "What?" There was even a blush. Mateo's stomach growled.

"I'm so goddamn lucky."

Sean's blush increased.

"Come here." Even Mateo heard the lust coating his words.

Sean tossed his towel aside and crossed the room. The moment he was within striking distance, Mateo snagged the man around the waist and pulled him into his lap.

"You look happy."

An evil smile tugged at the corners of Mateo's mouth at Sean's observation. He felt deadly. "I'm ecstatic. You're mine. All is right with the world." The deadly note to his voice didn't ebb.

Sean acted as if he didn't notice. "Are you nervous about your fight yet?"

Mateo shook his head. He couldn't think past the moment. "Right now, I'm focused on you."

Shifting positions in Mateo's hold, Sean came up onto his knees and pushed. Mateo gave him his way and fell onto his back. Sean flattened his palms against the mattress on either side of Mateo's head. The mischievous glint to Sean's eyes had Mateo's mouth going dry.

"I'm totally in love with you."

A surprised chuckle escaped Mateo. "I should hope so. If not, it'll be a long life for you. We have a good fifty or sixty years ahead of us."

Sean pinched him. "I'm telling you how I feel here."

"Okay. Okay," Mateo said, rubbing his side, trying to wipe away the sting of Sean's abuse. With a twist and a roll, he had Sean pinned beneath him. "Go on. Tell me how you feel. I need to hear how magnificent I am."

Sean huffed. "Never mind. You have a big enough head."

"Do I?" Mateo asked, sounding aroused even to his ears as he shifted positions, letting Sean feel his erection. "Tell me what you want, and maybe I can put this big head to use."

Sean smiled and shoved at his chest. "Let's play a game," he said, pushing his way out from underneath Mateo.

Mateo propped his head up with his fist and watched Sean cross the room. "I like games."

Sean dug through the welcome basket the casino had left in their room. He came out with a deck of cards. That got Mateo's attention. "You're not wearing enough for strip poker."

"We're not playing that," Sean said, climbing back in the bed. "This is our honeymoon and I want to know all your secrets. However, I'm willing to win them." He shuffled the cards while Mateo stared at him —bemused.

"Okay. Tell me the rules."

"It's simple," Sean said, setting the deck face down between them. "Whoever draws the higher card wins. Aces are high." He flipped the first card. It was a Jack. Mateo flipped a five. "You win," Sean said, smiling. "You get to ask the first question."

Even though this wasn't what Mateo had in mind for the night, he liked this idea. "All right. Did you always want to be a chef?"

Sean shrugged. "Not really, but I'm good at it, and it's a job." He flipped another card. It was a Queen. Mateo braced himself for anything. A triumphant-sounding hoot left him when he drew an Ace.

"What did you hope to be when you grew up?" Mateo asked, sticking with his theme.

A shy smile touched Sean's lips. "I thought about becoming a counselor, but then I realized I don't like most people I meet."

That confession surprised a laugh from Mateo.

Sean acted as if he liked everyone. Mateo drew another card. He drew a six. Sean pulled an eight.

"Finally. What's the craziest thing you've ever done?"

Mateo snorted. "You're not starting out light, I see. Hmmm, okay. When I was sixteen, my parents sent me to pick up my little brother from baseball."

"Wait," Sean said, waving his arms. "You have a little brother?"

The smile melted from Mateo's face. He tried not to think of Luis. "Yes, but tonight is a happy night, so ask me about him another time, okay?"

Sean nodded, looking solemn. "Okay. Continue."

"So, I went to pick up Luis and his practice ran long. So I grabbed my board and decided to film myself grinding the rail at the middle school field. It's super high. Anyhow, what I ended up filming was me breaking my leg."

Sean's laugh made the confession worthwhile. "I cannot picture you grinding a rail."

Mateo's cheeks heated. He still couldn't believe he'd confessed that. "Draw a card." Sean lost. Mateo mentally rubbed his hands together. "What's your favorite sexual position?"

Sean's face flushed red, making Mateo's smile grow. "Um." Sean pursed his lips, as if really thinking things over. His face screwed up. "You know, I don't think I have one. I'm pretty content with whatever you do to me."

"We'll see," Mateo said with a wink, flipping over another card. He lost.

Sean beamed. "The night we met, did you even really look at me before deciding to ask for my number?"

An inner groan rang through Mateo's head, but he was always honest with Sean. "No."

Sean nodded, as if he wasn't surprised. "Then why did you ask?" He paused. "Oops, I guess that's two questions." Sean reached for a card.

Mateo set his hand on top of them, stopping him. "You don't need this. Ask me anything. I'll answer. No, I didn't look at you. I smelled you. Your cologne brushed over me and your sweet voice called to me. Honestly, I didn't care about your appearance. Looks mean very little to me. Your being sexy is just a bonus. I fell so fast and hard for you, baby. I—"

Sean shoved the cards aside and straddled Mateo's hips. "You're the most amazing thing that's ever happened to me," Sean said before his lips came down on Mateo's hard. He was more than happy to let Sean take charge. As much as Mateo liked being in control, he couldn't pretend he didn't love the sensation of a man straddling his hips and riding his dick. Sean pushed at his underwear; Mateo lifted, letting him have them. Mateo kept busy too, peeling Sean's underwear down his body. He couldn't get inside Sean fast enough to suit his half insane mind. They were the only thing that kept him going. Not his career or training. Those things had kept him from walking into traffic for years, but the man in his arms—he was Mateo's salvation. Being Sean's husband was everything.

As only the second boxing match Sean had attended, he made an important discovery. He'd never get used to his husband getting hit. Sean wasn't a violent person. Every time a blow landed from Mateo's opponent, he wanted to storm the ring. His mom already held the back of his shirt as if reading his mind. Each round felt like forever. He didn't understand scoring, so he had no clue who was winning, but they were both bleeding. Each time Sean thought he'd settled down, giving his mom a chance to wave her sign and scream at the top of her lungs, Mateo would take a hit. Sean's dad was taking up the slack. He hadn't stop yelling since Mateo entered the ring.

The match was set for twelve rounds. They'd already gone eight and Sean wasn't sure he'd survive it.

He'd seen Aden, Remy, Daniel, and Isaac before the fight began, but he hadn't looked away from Mateo since. The four men could be right next to him for all he knew. All Sean knew was he needed this shit to end.

A bell rang and Mateo went to his corner. He could see his opponent's mouth moving—like he was talking shit—but Mateo didn't appear bothered.

They cleaned Mateo's cuts. Sean's dad said something about Mateo having the dude scared, but Sean was so sick to his stomach, he couldn't hear a thing. The bell rang again. Mateo nodded at whatever his cornerman said. He stood, moved to the center of the ring, and swung. His glove connected. Mateo's opponent, Cutter Wilson, went down on one knee. The count began but was over quickly when Cutter shifted back to his feet. Mateo threw another left jab, connecting once more. This time, Cutter swayed backward. Mateo held still, making Sean wonder if he held his breath. Cutter went down hard. The count started again. The bell rang. A cheer erupted. Sean stood—transfixed.

Daniel's arm found Sean's waist. "Let's go. They'll clean him up and he'll have a press conference. I'll get you in."

Sean let Daniel maneuver him through the crowd, but his gaze stayed locked on his husband. His arms were raised in victory. He'd won. Sean was so goddamn proud, he thought he might burst. It seemed as if he should be smiling, but Sean was numb. His feelings ran so deep, he couldn't dredge up a reaction. Too late, he remembered his parents. He glanced over his shoulder to find them on his heels. The noise of the crowd didn't die away as Daniel flashed a badge at security and pulled them into a separate room. The place was every bit as packed. There was a long table and a podium up front. Sean found himself squished against the wall as reporters filed in and filled the folding chairs.

"It'll be quick," Daniel assured him. "They'll want him out here before it becomes a security nightmare in the hall."

Sean kept nodding, not knowing what else to do. A door behind the table opened. Aden and Mateo spilled out, accompanied by several yellow-shirt security men. Aden spoke first. Sean didn't hear a word. His gaze never left his husband. He wanted to rush the podium and check his injuries for himself. Even though— logically—he knew everything moved along quickly, it felt like it took ages.

Mateo moved to the podium. Sound rushed back to his senses. People hurled questions Mateo's way. He searched the room with his gaze. When his stare landed on Sean, Sean's smile finally made an appearance. The love of his life had seen his biggest dream come true. There were no words.

Mateo motioned toward the nearest yellow shirt. "Would you escort my husband and in-laws up here before they're trampled? Thanks."

Everything felt surreal—like it happened to someone else. Security kept him pressed to the wall before he was shuffled behind the podium. Mateo's lips brushed Sean's before Aden helped him into one of the many chairs behind the table. His parents were given the same treatment. Mateo answered questions like a pro while Sean tried catching up. Mateo held everyone captivated, especially Sean.

"Mateo, Landon Shelby, *Boxing Today*, can you tell me where you went differently in this fight than you have in the past?"

Mateo chuckled. Sean had to take a breath. He loved that sound. "I won."

Even though Landon laughed along with everyone else, he didn't let up. "Is there anyone who helped you finally push past that barrier that's been holding you back from the title?"

"A lot of people have helped me along the way," Mateo said without hesitation. "Obviously, I never would've made it this far without my trainers, Aden and Remy. But I had zero chance at winning without my cheering team—my husband, Sean, and his parents, Robin and Scott."

Cameras flashed, blinding Sean. He tried to keep smiling. He didn't want anyone to think he wasn't every bit as proud as he was.

Someone else caught Mateo's attention. "Mateo, Leon Wright, *Las Vegas Fight Times*, I noticed your cornerman said something to you right before the ninth round began. Can you tell us what advice he gave?"

Mateo's smile was everything. "He said, knock the fucker out."

Mateo pointed at a woman in the back who'd been trying to get a question in. "Lynn Plumber, *Las Vegas Channel Ten*. What was your parents' reaction to the news?"

Mateo didn't miss a beat. "I have no parents." He called for the next question before anyone could call him on his statement. Sean didn't hear anything else. His heart fell. Mateo had finally given up. His heart shattered for all the pain his husband kept inside and never shared with anyone—not even him.

*T*he kitchen was booming with too many bodies in too small of a space. If Mateo hadn't already been leaving for the gym that morning, Sean might've called in. He was getting greedy with Mateo's time. If he didn't have Slip to distract him, Sean might scare himself a little when it came to his sexy husband. When they'd come home from Vegas, he'd expected their life to change with all the limelight, but nothing had really changed. It was like winning a trophy while playing any sport. Life didn't take away the accomplishment, but neither did it stop moving.

"Clock out and come to my office," Boston said, keeping his voice low enough for Sean's ears as he passed behind him through the kitchen. Since Sean had only been at work for fifteen minutes, the order sent his heart rate through the roof. Boston was always serious, except when it came to his husband, but this was more. Sean didn't think he'd done anything wrong.

After clocking out, Sean pulled off his black "Slip" chef's jacket. He found Boston sitting behind his desk. "What's up?"

Boston turned his laptop for Sean to see. "You might want to read this."

Sean's gaze slid to the screen. He spotted a picture of Mateo at his press conference and another of Mateo's parents. A sick sense of dread rose inside Sean. He moved closer to the screen and sat.

Two weeks ago, the boxing world welcomed a new Super Lightweight champion—Mateo Sousa. During his press conference afterward, Sousa shocked more than a few people when asked about his parents. He claimed he had none. Curiosity piqued, I decided to set out in search of these non-existent parents and found Renato and Izabella Sousa. Renato, a successful acquisitions agent, and Izabella, a well-known antique collector, were surprised to learn they did not exist.

"We tried reaching out to Mateo the day before his match," Renato tells us. "Our calls were ignored." Izabella had more to say than her husband. "Mateo hasn't been the same since his brother, Luis, was killed eight years ago."

Most people might remember eight years ago when eighteen-year-old Luis Sousa was brutally beaten to death outside a Miami nightclub. Luis, an openly gay college student, was lured outside by an unknown assailant where at least two other men were waiting. He was found an hour later in a side alley—unresponsive. According to Mateo's parents, after Luis' death, Mateo stopped coming around and their relationship fell apart. Both parents agree, Sousa's recent marriage to Sean Underwood was only more of the same—another way to pay penance for his guilt over his brother's death. Mateo had taken Luis to that club the night he was killed. "Sean is very much like Luis," Izabella says. "They both are quiet, sweet, and accustomed to abuse."

Sean couldn't read another word. "What the hell is this bunch of bullshit?" Sean roared, surprising even himself.

"Welcome to fame," Boston said, sounding resigned. "You probably need to find your husband. I can't imagine this is sitting well. The first public attack by the media is always the worst."

Sean didn't hesitate moving to his feet. "Thank you. I'm sorry about this. Mateo's parents are horrible, but I didn't expect..." Sean said, waving toward the laptop at a loss for words. "This," he finally said, because nothing else he thought to say should be said in polite company.

"Go," Boston said, waving him away.

With a nod, Sean headed for the parking lot. His heart hurt. He hadn't known about Luis. Mateo had never said a word, and things had been so crazy, he'd forgotten to ask about Mateo's mention of a brother. Sean remembered the news story, though. It had reaffirmed his hatred of going to nightclubs alone.

In his car, Sean's hands shook. He waffled between heartbroken and enraged. Even when Sean had practically run away and cut his parents from his life, they hadn't given up on him. They damn sure hadn't tried humiliating him. Mateo must be so upset. He had to find him. A quick pass by the house showed he wasn't there. Sean headed for the gym. His panic rose by the second. He didn't see Mateo's Jeep, but Sean went inside just in case.

Remy met him at the door. "He's not here," Remy said before Sean asked. "You missed him by five minutes."

"Shit," Sean said, running his hands through his hair. "How did this happen?"

Remy rubbed Sean's arms, obviously hoping to calm him. "Come sit down in Aden's office. You can call him and calm down before driving again."

Call him. Fuck. Why hadn't he done that first? It was like his brain didn't want to work. "Okay," Sean said, letting Remy lead him to Aden's office.

His gaze landed on Daniel and the man headed his

way. Sean thought about screaming he didn't want to deal with anyone right now, but his throat wouldn't work.

Daniel followed him in the office. "I'm working on a counter article to fix this," Daniel said, sounding genuinely concerned.

"Thanks, Daniel." Even to Sean's ears, he sounded dead. Nothing would be right again until he spoke to Mateo.

Remy flashed Daniel a sweet smile, making up for Sean's inability to cope. "Thanks, Daniel," he said, repeating Sean's words before closing the door. "I know this feels like the end of the world right now, but there'll be a new scandal next week and everyone will forget this."

Sean nodded, letting Remy know he was listening as he snagged the first chair he came to, and dialed Mateo's number. It went straight to voicemail. Sean left a message. "Teo, call me and let me you're okay. Love you."

He immediately tried a second time with the same result. "Goddamn it," Sean growled, resisting the urge to throw his phone. He stood. "I have to find him."

"You need to take a breath," Remy said, pushing him back down. "If you get into a wreck and kill yourself, you won't do Mateo any good."

Sean sucked in a deep breath through his nose.

"This is a nightmare." He took another breath. "Mateo says you used to be a title holder. Have you ever been through anything like this?"

Something dark passed over Remy's features, making Sean's heart squeeze in his chest. Remy was such an amazing person. He couldn't imagine anyone saying anything horrible about him. "Yes," Remy said, shocking Sean. "Winning the title was one of the worst things to ever happen to me. I worked hard for it and wouldn't trade my life for anything, but it also destroyed my life. Having your life under a microscope isn't for everyone. Can I tell you a secret?"

Sean nodded. He needed to focus on something else.

Remy's chest expanded before he spoke. "The night I lost the title, I threw the fight. All I wanted was Aden. I couldn't have both."

Sean's heart wouldn't slow. The barely suppressed panic inside him was clawing at his brain. "Why?" he asked, trying to hold on to his end of the conversation.

Remy stared at him for so long, Sean didn't think he'd answer. When he did, Sean's heart finally slowed, and he felt the first real connection to someone other than Mateo—like Remy could be his friend. "Aden is a recovering addict. He can't handle the stress of the fame. Also," Remy said, sounding as if the confession killed him as he added, "The longer I held the media's attention, the higher the risk of them finding out he cheated on me with Boston."

Sean's mouth fell open. He immediately snapped his teeth together. The last thing he wanted was to hurt Remy's feelings by showing his shock. He tried, but he couldn't hide it. "Aden and Boston? Seriously? But you're amazing and Boston loves Kaz."

Remy waved a dismissive hand. "This was back before Boston met Kaz, and—like I said—Aden is a recovering addict. He was high at the time. It's water under the bridge, but it killed me, and if it had been aired to the world, maybe I wouldn't have survived it."

Sean could see that. "They implied Mateo might be abusive," Sean said, feeling his rage build, but also a little better for having said it. He couldn't stop. "He's the best husband on the planet. Mateo saved me from the black hole where I stayed in my mind. And his brother, oh my god. He must be gutted right now. Why do the best people get all the bullshit while the pieces of shit in the world get all the luck? You should see his parents' house. It's obvious they've never wanted for a thing. And who attacks their own child like that?" Everything inside Sean poured out. "I went there, you know? Before Mateo's fight. I begged them to go—to support Mateo." Sean stood again. "I have to find Mateo."

"Okay," Remy said, letting him go this time. "At

least promise me you'll call me and let me know when you find him or when you're home safely?"

Sean nodded. "Of course. If you see him first, please let me know."

Remy nodded. Before he could stop himself, Sean hugged him, making Remy coo. "Awww, I knew we would be besties."

"Thank you," Sean whispered, hoping he didn't lose his shit before he found his husband.

———

THE THIRD FLOOR of his house had always been his favorite. Several times, Mateo had considered moving his bedroom here. It was nothing more than one large room with a small bathroom, but the view was amazing. One wall was all glass, giving him the perfect view of the water. Two things stopped him. It got hot as hell up here at night and he loved the shower in his bedroom. Since he hadn't moved his bed up here, he'd turned the floor into sort of an entertainment room. He could host a small dinner on the balcony or people could lounge around in one of the many chaises and comfortable chairs spread throughout the room.

When he needed peace, it was where Mateo went. Something about the water soothed him. Maybe because it made him feel insignificant. If he was a small cog in the universe, then so too were any problems he was having. Right now, he needed a blank mind. That damn newspaper article. It had implied so many horrible things, Mateo didn't know where to start ranting against it. He shouldn't have been surprised. His parents been enraged since he'd started seriously dating Sean, and then he'd married him in the most public way possible, and then he'd won the title.

The water wasn't helping today. He still wanted to smash shit. His cellphone had already lost its life. Reporters had been calling all morning. Honestly, he might not have seen the article otherwise. Mateo snorted and shook his head. Aden. Remy. Daniel. They'd all tried warning him about the fame. Aden had a life lessons course for his members where Daniel gave mock interviews, teaching people how to safeguard their lives from the media. Remy gave lessons on dealing with the stress and focusing on the positive side of fame. It wasn't that he hadn't taken those lessons seriously. He just hadn't expected to ever win. Possibly that was his dad talking. All the times he'd been called a gatekeeper stuck with him, but he hadn't expected Sean. Sean was the real reason Mateo had won that title. He gave Mateo confidence and something to fight for. No way would Sean want him after this. Mateo had promised to love and protect him.

Loving him would never be an issue. Protecting him—Mateo had already failed at that.

"There you are."

Mateo's head whipped toward the stairs. He hadn't heard Sean arrive. Since the man wasn't supposed to get home until ten and it was barely two, he hadn't been looking for him. His hair stood in every direction and he looked like hell. Mateo's guilt shot through the roof. Still, he couldn't convince himself to move from his chair.

"Hey, baby. You're home early."

Sean didn't soften. "I've been trying to call you."

Mateo shrugged. "My phone is dead." It was true. Only he meant more than the battery.

"Jesus fucking Christ. I've made myself sick looking for you," Sean said, crossing the room and going down on his knees between Mateo's. He massaged Mateo's thighs. "Are you okay?"

Sean was so sexy. Mateo's heart skipped a beat while staring down at him. How could he destroy this amazing man by marrying him? "I'm sorry." He really was. "Why are you home so early?"

Sean's brow furrowed. "For you."

"Oh." He'd seen the article. Mateo hadn't even considered that. He hadn't exactly been thinking clearly since he read it. Mateo swallowed, wondering where to start. He didn't know how to make things right. Really. There was only one way, and Mateo didn't think he was strong enough. Still, he swallowed again and tried. "Maybe we should get a divorce."

Sean sat back on his heels, looking like Mateo had punched him. "You want a divorce?"

Mateo shook his head. Everything hurt. There was a real possibility he might cry at the thought alone. "I don't want you to feel trapped by me."

Sean slapped his thigh. Hard. It shocked Mateo speechless. He'd never seen Sean look more furious. "How fucking dare you use that word with me? I thought you loved me."

"I do," Mateo said, trying to get his bearings.

"Then fucking show it," Sean said, confusing Mateo even further. He thought he was showing it, but there could be no doubt Sean was furious.

"I don't—"

"You don't what?" Sean asked, not letting him finish. "You don't deserve to have your name dragged through the mud? You don't deserve shitty parents? Is that what you were about to say? That had better be what you were about to fucking say."

In truth, Mateo was afraid to say anything now. He'd never seen Sean angry. It was hot, but he still preferred his sweet Sean. "I don't know what to do."

Sean deflated. His shoulders fell, and the outrage drained from his face. "What do you want to do? Don't think about it. Just tell me the first thing that pops into your head."

"I want to go back to yesterday when I woke up holding you and we were just newlyweds, enjoying our life together." Mateo searched Sean's face, needing that back. "You're the best thing to ever happen to me. I just want a quiet, normal life with you."

Sean stood. He pulled his shirt over his head and unbuttoned his pants. Mateo watched in silence—unsure where things were headed. Sean pushed his jeans down his hips. "Come on," he said, sounding impatient. "It's yesterday morning. We were both nude." Sean peeled off his socks before taking off his underwear. Finally, he stood completely nude—hands on hips and waiting for Mateo to do the same. He wasn't hard. This obviously wasn't about sex. That didn't stop Mateo's hunger from growing.

Rather than stripping, as Sean ordered, Mateo shot forward in his seat and snagged Sean's hips. He towed the man forward and wrapped his lips around the man's cock. Sean's dick hardened in his mouth. Damn, he loved that. He loved the way he could transform Sean's body—make him respond. His fingers dug into the backs of Sean's thighs. He couldn't let up. His head bobbed as he played with Sean's dick—licking and swirling. Inches worked their way down his throat. His mind emptied of everything except pleasing his husband.

Reaching down, he set his erection free, palming himself as he sucked. Sean held his head. Moans filled the silence with delicious noise. He didn't tease or take mercy. This wasn't about play time. He wanted Sean's cum. If he couldn't please his husband sexually, then why get up tomorrow. A light switch flipped in his head, changing everything. Mateo had been beyond happy since the day he met Sean. Nothing had changed. He loved this man. Sean obviously loved him. Everything else was background noise. Mateo didn't care about anything other than giving Sean the perfect life he deserved. Being surly and pissed wasn't the way to Sean's heart. Sean hadn't come home saying a word about the actual article. He'd rushed home, worried about Mateo.

Mateo was letting them win. They wanted to drive a wedge between Sean and him. It wasn't happening. He pulled away, making Sean cry out in denial.

"Don't worry, baby. I'll take care of you." Mateo meant it in a thousand ways. He stood. "This isn't yesterday morning. Yesterday, we were in bed." Sean's eyes looked unfocused, but he let Mateo lead him toward the stairs. He hoped Sean was thinking about yesterday morning—how Mateo had pressed him into the bed on his stomach and fucked him slow. He was about to do it again.

Mateo knew he'd won when they reached the bedroom and Sean sprawled out on the bed facedown, accepting of his fate. After stripping, Mateo opened the bedside table, found the lube, and coated his cock. He spent a minute enjoying the sensation of his oiled palm stroking his dick while he eyed his sexy, nude husband. Sean had the perfect ass—round and firm. Mateo loved spreading those cheeks and fucking that hole.

Having tortured himself enough, Mateo climbed on top, kneeing Sean's thighs apart as he went. Sean was so goddamn compliant. He didn't make a sound as Mateo rubbed his cock between the man's ass cheeks, enjoying the friction. He spread them wide and fingered Sean's asshole. Damn, Sean was perfect. Already his greedy ass pulled at Mateo's fingers like it was his dick. Mateo fisted his cock and positioned himself against Sean's hole. He pushed past the ring of muscles and retreated before doing it again, teasing Sean. Plus, he loved watching his cock penetrate Sean's ass. The sight of his crown disappearing inside Sean made him feel connected. He was playing witness to them becoming one person. His body screamed for release, warring with his mind that wanted to play all day. Mateo rolled his hips and went deep as he covered

Sean's body with his. His tongue automatically sought the inside of Sean's ear. He wanted to lick every place he could reach. His teeth sank into the man's lobe, drawing a moan.

He changed angles, hitting the spot inside Sean he knew would make the man come without ever touching his dick. "Damn, I love fucking you. Your body molds to mine. Your asshole refuses to let me go, tugging on my meat with every thrust. It's like you're a fucking magician." Sean gasped. Mateo was in his stride. "I want to make you come and then keep going to see how long you'll beg me to stop before you're coming all over our sheets again." Mateo pumped harder. He was so close. Sean cried out. His asshole squeezed tight before the spasms hit, keeping time with his jets of cum. Satisfaction roared through Mateo. He'd done that. "That's it, baby. Make a mess and suck my dick with your ass. You're so fucking hot. Goddamn, I'm so proud to be your husband. Fuck," Mateo gasped as the first spasm hit, the pressure turning to pleasure. "I'm going to fill your ass with cum all day. You're not leaving this bed. Don't worry; I'll lick your ass and keep it from getting sore."

"Teo," Sean gasped, stealing Mateo's breath. He didn't give a shit about anything. Sean filled every space. As he collapsed and rolled, bringing Sean with him, Mateo wondered why he'd been so upset earlier.

Sean had promised to love him forever. This was unbreakable.

SEAN REFUSED to let Mateo leave the bed for anything other than life's necessities. They needed this time to regroup after his parents' attack. Sean needed time to show Mateo he was loved. He loved Mateo enough for four people. Mateo would never feel a lack where his parents should be if Sean had anything to say. Most of their time together went uninterrupted. Mateo's phone was smashed beyond repair and they didn't have a house phone. Not many people had Sean's number, but a few people tried knocking on the door. They never looked to see who it was. Remy texted to check on them. Otherwise, they just spent a full twenty-four hours making love, kissing, or simply holding each other. They hadn't spoken about much. Sometimes there were no words. In this case, Sean could only show Mateo he would never be alone. Remy texted again, disrupting their cocoon.

Remy: *Tell Mateo to check out Daniel's article.*

Sean: *On it. Thanks.*

"Remy says you need to see Daniel's article." Sean hated saying those words. He was sick of dealing with the written word.

Mateo didn't seem to suffer the same fear of the media. He rolled to his side and pulled an e-reader from the bedside table. After scooting up on the bed and leaning his back against the headboard, Mateo scrolled for a minute before he handed the tablet to Sean. "Here. You can read it to me. My eyes hurt."

Sean accepted the device before crawling between Mateo's knees. He leaned against the solid wall of his husband's chest and read aloud. "In my journalism career, I've had a few occasions when I've come across an article by a peer where I've been horrified speechless. Usually, I stay quiet. Yesterday, I read one that finally crossed a line with me. It was a blatant attack on the new Super Lightweight boxing champion, Mateo Sousa. My offended sensibilities had nothing to do my friendship with Sousa, although I do like to think he considers me his friend. No, in this case, I was shocked by the tastelessness of such a respected newspaper as the *Boxing Report*. The *Daily Sports Report* doesn't make a habit of calling out other papers for false articles. This is a special case. In the face of massive evidence against their article and my personal knowledge of everyone involved, the chief editor of this fine paper has given me permission to print the truth."

Sean glanced over his shoulder. "Other than their underlying nasty implications, did your parents lie?"

"Oh, yeah," Mateo said with a telling look. "Keep reading."

Sean picked up where he left off. "While it's true Luis Sousa died a horrific death eight years ago, his older brother, Mateo, was in Las Vegas at the time of his death. If his parents had ever cared for him, they would've known he had his first main event match that weekend. While Luis was considered a sweet soul, this reporter doubts it's the reason for Mateo's recent marriage. Having personally met Sean, I'd describe him as more of a spitfire."

Sean chuckled. "I'll never live down that Christmas party."

"You were amazing," Mateo said, pressing a kiss to his temple.

Sean kept reading. "Additionally, the Sousas hadn't allowed any contact between the brothers since Mateo came out eleven years ago. Mateo hadn't seen or spoken to his brother for three years before his death. So, who are these people who stole the final years of sibling bonding from their sons? While I admit to not knowing much about Izabella Sousa, Renato Sousa is someone I know too much about. Mr. Sousa touts himself a collector of fine items on his website. He goes on to say there's nothing he can't acquire for the right price. Folks, he does mean anything.

"Last year, I had a mock interview with an up and

coming MMA fighter. During his visit to Key Largo, he had a visitor of his own at his hotel room—Renato Sousa. Renato had an outrageous offer. You see, this fighter has several gold medals and is very popular among MMA fans. It seems at least one of those fans would go to any length for one night in his bed. Renato hoped to buy this fighter's sexual favors for the night for an unnamed bidder."

"I wonder if Carter took the money," Mateo said with a chuckle, startling Sean.

"You know who he's talking about?"

He felt Mateo shrug against his back. "Sure. So do you. Do you remember the asshat who said I'd fuck anything that moved? That's him," Mateo finished before Sean could respond.

"Wow. That's nuts. Do you think your dad will sue him for this?"

"I don't know," Mateo said, sounding thoughtful. He leaned over Sean's shoulder. His gaze moved over the page before he settled back down. "It doesn't look like Daniel ever named him and reporters don't have to give up their sources. If anyone gets sued over this, I'll cover their legal fees."

"This was nice of Daniel and Carter, though it'll probably just fan the flames. Your dad will probably be here within the hour to yell at you."

"Nah," Mateo said, sounding sad. "After

yesterday's article, I left the gym and went straight to my lawyer's office. I filed a restraining order against him and had a letter drawn up, stating I'd sue them for slander if they came anywhere near any of us, including your parents. Also, if they accept any more interviews, I'll go after them for every penny. I paid a lot of money to have them served by the end of the day yesterday. Maybe I wouldn't win a case against them, but I'm sure enough people have witnessed their weekly tirades against me to lean things in my favor."

Even as a wave of relief washed over Sean, a hint of hurt crept in. "You have to stop hiding things from me, Teo."

Mateo shifted positions, taking the tablet from Sean's hand and setting it aside before repositioning their bodies until they were face to face on their sides. "Why do you think I hide things from you?"

The spark of hurt got a little bigger. "I didn't know about your brother's death until I read it in that article and you didn't say a word about restraining orders until just now. Sometimes, you make me feel like I'm living in the dark. You can talk to me. I love you. I want to help."

Mateo traced Sean's jaw with his fingertips. His expression was breaking Sean's heart. He looked lost. "It's my job to protect you. Even if that means keeping you safe from my family and my ugly past. You're a first for me, baby. I'm going to screw up occasionally."

"How do you mean I'm a first?"

Mateo's sweet smile hit Sean in the chest. "I've never been in love. No one has ever loved me. You'll have to cut me some slack when I don't know what I'm doing. After all, I'm doing the same for you."

Sean's brow furrowed. "What's that supposed to mean?"

Mateo shrugged. "You don't talk to me either, and you don't completely trust me. I'm worth millions, but you still work sixteen-hour shifts. You're afraid you'll eventually become a prisoner in our home if you quit. I get it. Even though I'm nothing like your ex, that fear still has to be real in your mind, but it still hurts my feelings."

Sean blinked. He didn't know what to say. In truth, he hadn't sat down and thought about it. Now that he was faced with Mateo's thoughts, he was kind of pissed. Sean shoved at Mateo's hard chest until he rolled onto his back. Sean straddled his hips and glared down at him. Mateo's smile didn't help cool Sean's temper one iota.

"I haven't quit my job because I signed a contract with Boston. He paid for my school so I have to continue working for him for the next three years or repay the money for my tuition. I also didn't want to assume you were cool with me mooching off you for the rest of my life. Not to mention, I don't give a shit about your money. It's yours. All I want is you. You're such an ass, ugh. You should fucking know all I care about is your time. If you were penniless and living in a box, I'd squeeze in there with you. Seriously, I'm so, so mad at you right now."

Mateo laughed, making things worse. "Are you sure you want me to stop hiding things from you?"

Sean barely stopped himself from punching Mateo in the crotch. "Yes." Even to his ears, Sean sounded petulant.

Mateo snagged Sean's wrists, confusing him. "You're wrong. It's not my money. It's our money." Sean realized how smart Mateo had been to hold his arms. He'd never wanted to punch another person as badly in his life. Sean fought against his hold. Of course, Mateo won.

"I really need to take Remy's boxing lessons more seriously. One of these days, I'll kick your ass, and you'll wonder why. Just look back and remember this moment."

Mateo rolled, pinning Sean beneath him. His laughter bounced off their bedroom walls. He couldn't remember the last time he'd seen Mateo laugh so loudly and openly. Sean fell still and stared. Until that moment, he hadn't realized how much Mateo had been silently enduring. Sean's eyes filled with tears. Mateo's laughter died.

He released Sean's arms. "Am I hurting you? I'm sorry, baby," he said, sounding panicked as he rubbed Sean's forearms where he'd been holding them.

Sean shook his head. "You weren't hurting me. I haven't seen you laugh in a long time. All I want is for you to be happy. I didn't realize how much I was failing until now."

Mateo relaxed into Sean, their bodies melding. "You're my only happiness. I've been failing myself by clinging to the people who gave me life. Most people get good parents, or at least parents who try. When you're the one who's drawn the shit straw and end up with parents like mine, it's hard to know what's right. Society teaches us to honor them. What do you do when they don't love you like normal parents would? It's hard for other people to understand. They can't fathom parents hating their children, so there must be something wrong with me."

Sean stroked Mateo's hair. Mateo was giving him what he'd asked for by opening up. Now Sean wanted to soothe it away. "There's nothing wrong with you."

Mateo nodded. "I know, but only because I met you. Before you, I just clung, trying to do better and be who they needed while never understanding what I did wrong. After all, if my parents couldn't love me, who could? I thought I was broken somehow. My grandmother tried to make me understand it wasn't me while lamenting over where she'd gone wrong with her son. She died before she could undo eighteen years of mental abuse." Mateo pressed his cheek to Sean's chest and tilted his chin up, meeting Sean's gaze. "Before we got married, you said I'd tell the story of our crazy wedding to our grandkids one day. When you said that, a shot of fear hit me. I realized then how scared I am of becoming like them. You're so nice and perfect. I don't ever want to steal that from you."

Sean snorted. He couldn't help it. "You realize we're just alike, right? Like—seriously—there aren't two people on the planet more suited for each other, because it's like we're the same person."

Mateo shook his head. "I'm nothing like you, but I'd like to be. You heard what Carter said about me the night we met. He wasn't just being an ass. I did a lot of stupid shit while searching for you."

A sigh rose in Sean's throat. Mateo saw him through such rose-colored glasses. "I was insulted that night, because I would've loved to have given you my number and he turned our moment into something ugly. That doesn't change the fact that I wanted to be seduced by you. How does that make you worse than me or me better than you?"

Mateo shrugged. "I probably wouldn't have called if you'd taken me home that night."

Sean's smile was out of his control. "I did take you home that night."

"Yeah, but nothing happened," Mateo shot back.

"How do you know? You passed out." Sean wanted to crow with laughter at Mateo's shocked expression. He waved his hand through the air, adding, "But, nonetheless, that's semantics. You did go home with me. You stayed the night, and you called the next day. I think—no matter what—you would've called. We would've ended up right here, and it would've happened, because we are meant to be."

"Wait," Mateo said, shaking his head. "What did happen that night?"

Devilry overtook Sean. He wrapped his arms around Mateo and urged him higher so he could claim the man's lips. He spoke between kisses. "I got you to wake up long enough to limp to the couch. Mhmm," Sean hummed as Mateo licked his bottom lip. He tried to keep going. "After getting you settled, I changed into a pair of shorts to sleep in, found you a blanket, and came back." Sean grabbed Mateo's hand and slid it down his body to his erection. "When I bent to cover you up, you shoved your hand inside my shorts with the speed of a very sober man."

Mateo pulled away. His expression called Sean a liar before his mouth had time. "Nu-uh."

Sean nodded. His breath caught at the back of his throat as Mateo kneaded his cock the same as he had that night. "I was shocked, to say the least, but I also couldn't bring myself to move away. You said, 'If I was sober right now, I promise you'd never forget me.' I almost came right then. You sounded that hot and confident. Instead, you passed out. I disentangled myself from your hold, covered you up, and went to bed to jack off."

A flush touched Mateo's cheeks. "You jacked off while I was one room away?"

Sean nodded.

Mateo released a loud breath. "Jesus, that's so fucking hot. I hate myself for drinking so much that night."

Sean shrugged. "I got off either way, and now you're my husband. You can make it up to me every night."

"Every night? That's a tall order. Sometimes I'm tired."

A burble of laughter escaped Sean. It died on a moan as Mateo's hand dipped between his legs.

"I can try for every night, though. We might have to get inventive. Forever is a lot of nights."

"We got this," Sean said, lifting his hips and taking what he wanted from Mateo's fingers. "Like I said, we're fucking perfect together. We don't need anyone or anything else. We can make forever our bitch." They would too because a love like theirs was too strong to ever let anything break them. Since they'd met, no one had as much as cracked their bond. It would be that way forever. Maybe even beyond.

ABOUT THE AUTHOR

Charity Parkerson is an award winning and multi-published author with several companies. Born with no filter from her brain to her mouth, she decided to take this odd quirk and insert it in her characters.

*2015 Readers' Favorite Award Winner

    *Winner of 2, 2014 Readers' Favorite Awards

    *2015 Passionate Plume Award Finalist

    *2013 Readers' Favorite Award Winner

    *2013 Reviewers' Choice Award Winner

    *2012 ARRA Finalist for Favorite Paranormal Romance

    *Five-time winner of The Mistress of the Darkpath

Connect with her online:

--Join my street team: facebook.com/TeamCharityParkerson

--Sign up for my newsletter: http://bit.ly/CharityNews

--Website: charityparkerson.com

--Facebook: facebook.com/authorCharityParkerson

facebook.com/TheMenofSin

--Twitter: twitter.com/CharityParkerso

www.charityparkerson.com

admin@charityparkerson.com

www.ingramcontent.com/pod-product-compliance
Lightning Source LLC
Chambersburg PA
CBHW061232170626
46809CB00007B/2633